Tawnee Chasny

Ting!

The Silent Warning

Ting! The Silent Warning © 2021 Tawnee Chasny

All rights reserved. No part of this publication may be reproduced, distributed, or transmitted in any form or by any means, including photocopying, recording, or other electronic or mechanical methods, without the prior written permission of the publisher, except in the case brief quotations embodied in critical reviews and other noncommercial uses permitted by copyright law.

ISBN:

Paperback	978-1-954341-85-2
E-book	978-1-63945-135-7

The views expressed in this book are solely those of the author and do not necessarily reflect the views of the publisher, and the publisher hereby disclaims any responsibility for them.

Writers'
BRANDING

Writers' Branding
1800-608-6550
www.writersbranding.com
orders@writersbranding.com

CONTENTS

CHAPTER 1 1
CHAPTER 2 13
CHAPTER 3 19
CHAPTER 4 35
CHAPTER 5 51
CHAPTER 6 59
CHAPTER 7 71
CHAPTER 8 79
CHAPTER 9 89
CHAPTER 10 101

EPILOGUE FIVE MONTHS LATER 119

To my hubby, Kennar, for the great editing job and putting up with me. To my daughter who is my best friend, for her encouragement. To my son, for his love always.
I give to you the "Tings" you need in life.

~<]:o) Love y'all.

CHAPTER 1

Lilly came upon it quite by accident, as she did with many of the things she collected. Her mind was wandering as she strolled through the trees on her way to "The Village." The path was of hard packed dirt pounded down by more animals than people. Gramps had told her that it was a "deer trail," one of the easiest ways to find your way through the forest. The animals never get lost here, and they know the best way to get from here to there without being disturbed by people. She loved the peace and quiet that she found here and nowhere else. In her youth, she'd spent most of her summers here in the mountains with her grandparents.

"The Village" is a fairly large store on the ground floor of a very large, two-story log cabin. The owner George Foster, his wife Kelly, and their five boys live upstairs. George's father, George Senior, inherited the cabin from his Uncle Mathews, and he in turn passed it along to his son and daughter-in-law when they had but one child.

"Heck, son, you're more into living off the land like your Ma than I am. Why don't you take Kelly and the baby there and raise your family in God's country. We'll come up as often as we can, it's only a couple hours' drive from here. It's not like we're sending you away."

It was built, some say, long before the turn of the century. It was located not too far from her own cabin. About a twenty-minute walk. They had a small deli and a bakery shop (homemade—Kelly's department) in the back of the store. Up front it had just about everything you needed, from hardware, small tools like hammers, screwdrivers, nails, screws, and assorted sundries. There was also a small souvenirs corner operated by Zelda Compton. Driving there was out of the question. A walk in the woods was just what Lilly's mood required. She needed to buy a few things because she was making a special dinner for her new friend tonight.

She had met her new friend Joanne at her neighbor Howard Bluefeather's house during one of her visits to deliver an item that she had made for them. Howard and his two oldest sons, Jason and Daniel, had helped Joanne move into the house that Ken and Tillie Johnson had moved out of a few months ago. She was there visiting when Lilly arrived. Lilly and Joanne liked each other right away. She invited the woman over to her house for dinner so that they might get better acquainted and to welcome her to the neighborhood, if you could call it that in the mountains.

Out of the corner of her eye, she saw a flash of bright blue light. *Mmm! That's curious.* When she approached the spot where she thought she saw it, there was nothing to be seen but a large tangle of blackberry vines. She smiled to herself thinking about the rabbit in an old fairytale that was begging not to be thrown in the "briar patch." *Clever little guy, wasn't he?* she said aloud to herself. Curious, she got as close as she could without getting pricked or snagged by the wicked thorns. She pulled her long chestnut hair away from her face, holding it out of the way, and peered beneath the vines. *Nothing here. Must have been my imaginings again. And no rabbit hole either.* As she turned to be on her way, the most beautiful flash of green light caught her attention. *Hum! I thought it was blue. Maybe there's more than one of these . . . whatever they are.* Then she spotted it. Wedged amidst three large vines was what appeared to be a large piece of glass about the size of her hand. As she moved about trying to see it better, the reflection caught the sunlight at different angles. Each flash of light a different color. Fire red, sky blue, emerald green, and all the colors between. Each appeared to have its own source of light from within itself.

She had always had a talent for making beautiful things out of the most ordinary, sometimes odd objects. Her cabin was full of them. She had given several away to admiring friends. "If you really like it that much, you can have it."

Zelda, the owner of the "Curio Shopio" in "The Village," displayed and sold some of Lilly's things for her. Zelda even came over to Lilly's cabin and took pictures of her "masterpieces" as Zelda called them. These were now in an album/catalog set on the counter for customers to look through and possibly make a purchase. Without that, her table would be rather bare at times. Now there were people asking her to make things on special order. A friend of a friend had seen her work in various places and asked about her doing something special for them.

Searching around, she found a stick *just* long enough to reach this colorful thing. Parting the vines carefully, she could just barely touch it. It seemed to be wedged rather tightly. *Perhaps I can get the stick underneath and loosen it.* She pressed the pointed end under the glass and pressed down on the other end of the stick. WHOOSH! It went flying into the air, landing on the path where she had been walking. *That was lucky. It could have been lost and never found with all these ferns and bushes around here.* She returned to the path and picked it up. It was light as a feather, but just large enough that she couldn't close her fingers all the way around it. As she turned it in her hand, the colors seemed dull, almost colorless. *Mmm! Maybe just the way it caught the light.* The edges were irregular, almost sharp, but not enough to cut. The shape was roughly that of a large egg, but flattened like a river rock. Being in a hurry, she stuck it in her knapsack and continued along the path to The Village market.

. . .

After dinner, she served blackberry cobbler with sweet creme. "Lilly! This is so delicious. Where did you get berries this nice around here? I didn't see any in the market."

"I found them in the forest on my way home from the store. Which reminds me. I found something else today that I might be able to use somehow. Come on, Joanne, let's go in the other room, the light's better in there anyway. Bring your bowl with you."

"Don't worry! I'm not letting go of this bowl until it's empty."

. . .

The "other room" was her workshop. She had all kinds of hand tools, rolls of wire, various colors of paint, brushes, spray cans, small glass and plastic jars containing different sizes of screws and nails, and boxes of ordinary and oddly shaped objects. All of this was somewhat neatly arranged on shelves and hooks that were mounted on the wall. There were projects near finished, and just being started lying about on three tables that lined one whole wall. Two articles setting on newspaper looked as if they were finished and waiting for the paint and glue to dry. "This stuff is beautiful. You're really are good at what you do. I don't think my pinkie finger has the talent you do." She strolled around the room, eating and making a close inspection of everything she could see, careful not to touch anything. "Some of these pieces should be in an art showing. I've seen some of the things they call art, and they aren't as good as these unfinished ones. These are wonderful! You could make a fortune!"

"I just can't survive in the big city and I don't want to do business there either. In fact, I grew up in the city and it's not for me. I almost lost my creative edge there and I'm just now getting it back. Thank you for the compliment, but I don't do this for money. Well! Yes, just enough to live on. I don't get my inheritance for another year, when I'm twenty-five. Guess my grandparents wanted me to mature a little before I got the money. I'm glad they did. I've learned a lot since leaving home."

"So if you don't mind my asking, are you going to be rich?"

"Not really. It will be enough to keep me comfortable, not work and let my time be free to be creative. My grandparents told me uncountable times, 'Never give up your God-given talent, child. The Good Lord gave it to you for a reason. So don't waste it.'"

"Fact is this used to be their cabin. I moved out here when my parents, *who got very little by the way,* started making plans for my inheritance. I was only seventeen. I had to go to court. I was granted emancipation. I finished my education by mail. My teachers were upset but understanding about my leaving. They would send a package of books and lessons. When I returned the books, they sent me tests to be taken on the lessons I just returned. And of course more books for my next lessons. I finally finished my primary education through high school. It took two years, but I did it."

"Well! You are a smart one. That took a lot of dedication. But if you don't have to ever work, why bother?" Joanne asked.

"I did it for myself. It's hard for me to leave things unfinished," Lilly said, her shoulders pulled back with pride.

"Congratulations, Lilly. You have something to be proud of."

"Well enough about me. I ramble on so. Not many visitors come this far out. I like it that way. It's so peaceful here, I can get a lot done without interruptions. Don't get me wrong. I enjoy a visitor now and then. But I enjoy my privacy too."

"No offense taken. I understand perfectly. I believe we're going to get along just fine." Joanne smiled. "I'm trying to get away from people too, maybe not for the same reasons, but I too enjoy my solitude. So many people, kids, husband's friends, my dress shop, the people working for me, there was no time for myself. Don't get me started. I'm babbling again."

Lilly picked up her knapsack and fished for the piece of glass she found earlier. In the process, she removed two other items and placed them on her workbench. "Ahh! Here it is," she said and held it out for Joanne's inspection. "It was much more colorful out in the sunlight."

"Oh my!" Joanne said as Lilly placed it in her hand. "This is really light. It weighs hardly anything at all, for as big as it is. You think it might be plastic? It's kind of dull, maybe you can polish it somehow. Whatever will you make out of this?"

"I'm not sure what it's made out of, and I'm never sure what I'm going to do with any of these things," she said, gesturing with her hand at everything in general around the room. "I just collect what I find, store them away, and then ideas come to me later. Sometimes people give me odd things that they have found. 'Thought of you when I saw this. Maybe you could make something out of it.' I have quite a collection. See?" she said as she pulled open a couple of large drawers at the bottom of the workbench.

"Wow! Looks like you're going to be real busy. It's hard to tell what some of this stuff is."

"Yes, I know. I've never thrown anything away that someone has given me. You never know when you might use something that looks like junk," Lilly told her. "I keep the larger items in the storage shed out back."

Handing the piece of glass back to Lilly and looking at her watch, Joanne said, "I'm sure that you'll figure out something to do with this. I must be enjoying myself. Time is really flying by, and it's late. I hope you won't think I'm unkind, but I've got to be going. I've got to get up early and drive into town for a dentist appointment in the morning."

"Not at all. I'm very happy to have had you over for dinner."

"And don't forget you're having dinner at my house next week," Joanne reminded her. "I'll call you when I figure out which day would be best. Now let's clean up the dishes and I'll be on my way."

"That's not a problem. I'll take care of it. There isn't that much to do."

"Then it will only take half the time if I help," Joanne said as she headed out of the workshop and started clearing the kitchen table.

"This is very kind of you." Lilly smiled.

"Just wait till you have dinner at my house. I'm a messy cook. You'll see, I usually end up wearing at least part of dinner before it's served. Now that I'm a bachelorette, I usually eat over the sink, out of the pot."

They had a pleasant chat while finishing the dishes, and Lilly walked Joanne out to her car. "Call me when you get home so I'll know that you got there OK."

"That's nice of you. I'll do that. Thanks for your concern. Bye now."

"Bye! Bye now. Drive carefully, these mountain roads aren't like the city streets."

Lilly waved good bye from the porch and watched her new friend's taillights disappear. When she returned to the house, she started closing everything up, locking the doors, and turning the lights off except for the one by her reading chair. She went into the kitchen to heat some water for tea. She opened the refrigerator and took a small portion of blackberry cobbler, which she finished before the water was ready. She rinsed the bowl and spoon and placed them in the rack to dry. The pot started to whistle and she poured hot water over the loose tea leaves in her cup. This was her favorite cup. She had made it for her grandmother several years ago. It was rather large and had "GRAMMY" written on the side, in better than typical young hand-printing. She was only thirteen when she made it in school. Her teacher gave her a "A" in art class for that and a few other things that she had made. Her talent was already developing at that young age, in drawing, painting, crafts, clay, and anything else that was given to her to do. She even took "wood working" in her junior year in high school.

Her classmates made fun of her for her choice. "That's for boys." A girlfriend of hers joined the class with her. "Well! If I can't handle the class, at least I'll have one class with mostly all boys. That's got to make certain people careful about how they treat their boyfriends, now that we're going to be so close to them. Some of the girls need a lesson in manners. Besides, my mom thinks it's a good idea to learn this stuff. She tells me, 'At least you won't be waiting around till some guy decides that the little lady needs help, but I'll do it when I decide it's time, not when she tells me.' She and Dad didn't get along too well. Lovely family I come from," she said with a wry smile.

The projects that she was given turned out so well that the guys were taking tips from her. Her teacher encouraged her to assist the other students when they asked. To her surprise, she had a lot of compliments from the girls and the boys in school. Again she received "As" in this class too. Two of her projects were put in the display case next to the office to show visitors and students alike what kind work could be done in that class.

. . .

Joanne arrived home ten minutes later. As she got out of the car, she noticed that another car had slowed to almost a stop in front of her driveway and then pull away, speeding off up the road. *I wonder who that was. I don't know the car.* She could see quite far from where she stood. The car disappeared over the crest of the hill about a half mile up the road. *Hum? That was strange. Maybe they're lost.* She turned and walked about twenty feet up the path to the front door of her "A-frame" house. Even though she had only been here three months, she really loved living here. "This is home, really home." She'd told herself more than once. The house was a real bargain. It cost less than what she had sold the old house for. She bought it from an older couple that wanted to move to Florida, because "the winters weren't as cold as they are up here with the snow and all." Traveling back and forth to spend the summers was a bit too much for them at their age.

Joanne retired early at age fifty-five. She had sold her house and her dressmaking business, she took her moderate nest egg, along with Carl's retirement and social security and almost *ran* away from the crowded city. Leaving it far behind, with no regrets. Her husband had passed away last year and she needed to get away from all the memories. Her two children were grown and had their own families. They lived where they worked in other states which made visiting difficult. She decided that if they had to travel to see each other anyway, then they could just as easily travel in this direction instead of that. Besides this is closer and a much better place to visit than the place she and their father had lived in for so many years. She had grown up in the mountains and had moved to the city when she was about Lilly's age. Shortly after arriving, she met and married Carl Mason and lived in the city ever since. Moving was never an option because of his work. Now she felt that she was back where she belonged, out here in God's mountains. Come spring she would plant all kinds of flowers and really dress the place up. The house was in good condition, but the yard needed some help. That was OK because she has a green thumb.

As she closed the door, she heard a car and looked out the window. It was the same one as before. Again, driving slowly past the house. She hadn't turned the inside lights on yet, so she stood there watching, knowing that she couldn't be seen behind the curtains. It pulled to a stop and just sat there, for almost a full minute. The light inside the car came on and it looked to her that whoever it was, was looking at a map or something. The light went off and it pulled away. *Humm! Maybe they are lost. I know that these mountain roads can be confusing if you're not used to them.* She breathed a little easier after convincing herself that she was right about them being lost. After all this wasn't the big city where you have to be cautious about all strangers.

She made a cup of tea and then remembered that she promised to call Lilly. "Hi, Lilly, this is Joanne. I made it home about fifteen minutes ago."

"Oh good. I was wondering how long it would take you to get home." "Well, I've made myself some tea, and I'm eating the cobbler that you sent home with me. I swear it kept saying. *'Eat me, pleeease eat me. You know you want to. Besides it's too cold in the refrigerator.'* So I gave in," she said and laughed.

Lilly laughed along with her and added, "Well, I'm delighted that you got home OK, and that I'm not the only one that's enjoying seconds of the cobbler. It was good, wasn't it? Hey! thanks for calling me."

"I'm sorry it took so long to call you, but . . ." Then she told Lilly about the car that drove by her house a couple times.

"Oh my! That was strange. Are you OK with being alone? Do you want me to call Sheriff Wilson? Let him know about this?"

"No, I'm OK. I'm almost sure that whoever it was, was lost. I think if they were trying to be sneaky, they wouldn't be so obvious.

"That *was* unusual, you'll have to admit," Lilly said with concern. "You're more than welcome to come back here if you feel uncomfortable about where you are . . . I could come over there."

"No! No! I'm just fine. I've got my husband's .357 and I know how to use it. If I need anything, I'll call. Thank you for being concerned. You make a good friend. Good night, dear."

"Well! If you're sure."

"Yes, my friend. I'll be just fine. I shouldn't have worried you with it. It's more than likely nothing at all. I still have my big city nerves working that's all. Good night, and thanks again for the lovely dinner."

"Well! OK! But remember to call if you need company. I'm not that far away," she assured her. "Hey! Maybe we could go target practicing some time."

"That could be fun. We'll take a picnic and make a day of it."

"Let's do that soon. OK?"

She smiled to herself. "Good night. I'll be calling you soon about dinner at my place."

CHAPTER 2

After talking with Joanne, Lilly settled into her grandfather's reading chair with the book that she had been reading. It was one of Dean Koontz's latest novels. She'd read most of them and really liked them. Some were real page turners. She picked up her tea and was about to take a sip when she heard . . .

"Ting."

She froze with the cup almost to her lips. *What?*

"Ting!"

What in the world? She stood and turned in place. Looking around, she saw nothing.

"Ting!"

Walking slowly toward where she thought the sound came from, she saw a light coming from under the door of her workshop. *I don't remember leaving the light on in there. What is that sound?* Easing open the drawer of the cabinet next to her, she pulled out her grandfather's 9mm Mauser and released the safety, approaching the workshop door.

TING! THE SILENT WARNING

"Ting!"

Steeling her nerves, she quickly pushed it open with her foot, gun ready. There on the workbench was the glass that she had found earlier. It was standing up on end spinning and flashing a rainbow of colors.

"Ting! . . . Ting! . . . Ting!"

She almost dropped the gun, she was so startled but she held on. Such a thing to see! The tinging sound was that of a small bell, or closer to the light tap of a spoon on the rim of crystal goblet and very pleasant to the ear. "Sooo!" she said. "You're enchanted," she whispered almost reverently, putting the safety back on and placing the gun on the workbench. As soon as she did, the glass fell silently to the table, but the colors remained. "Now what is this all about?" she asked.

"I come to you from the spirit of your grandfather."

"You didn't come to me. I found you in the forest," she challenged.

"Your path was predetermined."

"How is that possible?"

"Not when, but where. You have walked that path many times."

"Yes but . . ."

"Been there a couple of weeks. Did you like the blackberries?"

"Yes, but how did you know?"

"That is my function, to enhance quality. They were poorly grown and not yet sweet when I arrived. I enhanced them."

"They were very good. Why did you do this?"

"Your grandfather sent me to help with many things."

"From where and like what? What else do you do?"

"That is for to you to choose. If I can help, I will."

"I've never heard of such a thing happening. Can I talk to Grandpa?"

"Possibly . . . in time. There is something for you to remember."

"And that is? There's always a catch," she said sarcastically.

"Tell nobody, or I will leave this object and it will return to being nothing but an old piece of glass."

"Is that why Joanne didn't think much of you?"

"The glass is only a vessel for the power. It was only a piece of glass when I arrived here. I enhanced it and now it is crystal. I am for only you to have knowledge of. No one else can hear me or see my crystal quality."

"But that would be selfish for me to help *only* myself."

"Your wish to do for others is of yourself. If you are involved, I will help if requested."

Suddenly, Lilly felt very tired. It had been a long day, the walk to the village, cooking, visiting. "This is all a lot for me to absorb, and I'm tired," Lilly said, yawning and suddenly very sleepy.

"Then sleep, child. I'll be here when you awake."

"What do I do with you? I don't think it would be right to leave you just lying on the table."

"The knapsack was nice."

"OK," she said yawning and placed the glass in her knapsack and dropped it back on the floor. In the front room, she finished her tea and tried to read, but she was too sleepy. Besides the fact that her mind wasn't in the mood to read anymore. After locking up the house, she brushed her teeth, washed her face, and went to bed. She slipped easily into a dream of her grandpa. She loved him. They had a special bond when he was alive. It was a comforting thought that it wasn't broken by his passing.

. . .

"Hello, darlin'."

"Hi, Grandpa." She ran to him and threw herself into his arms. It felt so good to have his arms wrapped around her again. "I miss you so."

"We miss you too, sweetheart." She could see Grams sitting in the corner, and they looked at each other smiling. She waved hello and Grammy rocked in her chair and blew her a kiss off the tip of her fingers. Then her grandpa held her at arm's length and said, "I see you found the crystal, and that means you're not alone."

"You mean the glass?"

"Well! When it's active, it looks like a crystal."

"It's very pretty, and it makes a sound."

"We sent it to you to help you along when things get difficult. Like the blackberries."

"Well! I guess that's OK, but you know I like to do things in my own way."

"Take it from a wise old man, my li'l darlin'. Things aren't like they used to be. Life is getting more difficult for everyone. The crystal will not do things for you, but it will make things easier. The end results will be the same. It only works upon request, and it's not going to do anything it's not asked to do. The blackberries were just an example to demonstrate what it can do. It will turn off the fire in the oven, only if you ask it, to not let the cookies burn because you are busy and might forget."

"What else can it do?"

"Anything, short of returning life to the dead. You'll have to be the judge of what you ask."

"Well! I won't be wasting it on things I don't need help with."

"That's my girl. I know you won't. That's why I sent it to help you. We know how your parents are. You had it hard growing up. Now it's time for some small rewards."

"What's with the 'Ting' sound that it makes?"

"Oh! Yeah! You're the only person that can hear that. It's like the silent warning we hear before we say, 'I just knew something was going to happen,' or, 'I just felt it in my bones.' Remember that feeling? We've talked about it before."

"Yes! I do," she said slowly, thinking back.

"The crystal will help you hear it better. Your early warning system, among other things. The 'Ting' is good. It lets you know when things are OK. It also makes a 'Tong' sound as a warning."

"Warning?"

"You know that *feeling* you get when things aren't right? Remember the *silent warning* that we used to talk about?"

"Yes! It's almost like hearing but not quite."

"The crystal will let you hear a warning for sure. The 'Tong' lets you know when something is not what it should be. Telling you to *be careful*, there might be danger around. Maybe not what it is, but where you are, or what you are doing. It will not speak to you anymore, but will 'Ting' or 'Tong' in response to what you say or ask. Like 'Ting' for yes or good and 'Tong' for no, or be careful."

"Like what kind of danger?"

"For example, when you go on your little walk in the woods by yourself, there could be a wolf or wild cat that may harm you."

"That's comforting."

"I'm not saying that you are going to be in danger. I can't see into your future. This is just in case. I'm not there to protect you anymore. This is the main reason for the gift. Please take it with you, wherever you go. Promise me!"

"I will, Grandpa. I promise!" At that, she fell into a deep, restful sleep.

CHAPTER 3

When Lilly woke up in the morning, she felt good. Before getting out of bed, she stretched her arms, legs, toes, and neck as far as they could go and yawned wholeheartedly. Her grandpa used to say, "I'd would stretch a mile if I didn't have to walk back." She smiled at the thought. "Mmmm!" Then she just lay there. Suddenly her dream popped into her mind and then she sat straight up in bed, very much awake. She sprang out of bed and retrieved her knapsack. Fishing through it as she walked, she pulled out the crystal and headed for the kitchen table.

"Good morning," she said, setting it on the table.

"Ting."

She started a pot of coffee, made some oatmeal in the microwave, and sat down at the table. The crystal just lay there dull and apparently lifeless. "So! Tell me about yourself," she said.

"Tong."

"Oh, that's right, Grandpa said, hmmmm! I actually talked to him last night."

"Ting."

"Then it wasn't a dream. It was a vision," trying to reassure herself.

"Ting."

"Oh! I forgot to ask him about Gram. She was there with him. We waved at each other, but we didn't speak."

"Ting."

"I hope she doesn't think I've forgotten about her."

"Tong."

She poured herself some coffee and set the cup on the table. "I'll be right back."

When she returned, her hands were full and she put the things on the table. "Now let's see." She worked quickly, and in about thirty minutes, she had made a small pouch out of soft deer skin. On each side stitched with silver-colored thread was a beautifully embroidered wild flower. She had twisted several pieces of fine blue twine together and made a drawstring, which she threaded through the holes at the top of the pouch. Holding it up, she said, "This is your new home. Do you like it?"

"Ting."

"I'm supposed to take you everywhere I go, and sometimes I don't take my knapsack. I'll just tie the string to my belt."

"Ting."

"Let's see how it fits," she said, sliding the crystal inside the pouch (a perfect fit) and carried it into the bathroom and hung it on the doorknob while she took a shower.

"Ting!"

. . .

After showering and washing her hair, she went into the front room and curled up in Grandpa's chair and pulled the comforter around her legs against the chilly morning air. She brushed her long chestnut hair and let it hang loose to dry. On the side table, the phone rang. She picked it up. "Hello?"

"Good morning!" Joanne said. "Did you sleep well?"

"Mmm! Yes, I did," Lilly said. "Good morning. What's up?"

"I have something to show you, when you get the chance to come over. I just need an opinion on something, when you have the time. It's not urgent, but I thought that you might stop by if you're out and about today."

As she listened to her new friend talking, she detected a poorly camouflaged nervousness in her voice. "Of course. It's not a problem at all. I can come over now, *if you like.* I'm not doing anything special."

"That would be very nice of you, dear. I don't want to be a pest," she said, clearing her throat.

"Are you all right?"

"Oh yes! I'm fine!" she blurted out. "I'll explain my dilemma when you get here. I really appreciate your concern. I'm sure it's nothing, just odd, that's all."

"OK. I'm going to grab some toast, and I'll be right over."

"That's good, dear, I'll see you in a few minutes then. Thank you. Bye."

"OK. See you soon." Lilly hung up the phone, went into the kitchen, and put some bread in the toaster. While that was cooking, she went into the bedroom and put some warm clothes on. It was going to be chilly today. She found a pair of her usual jeans, a long-sleeved T-shirt, and a sweatshirt with a hood. Unless it got down to freezing temperatures, this is what she wore most of the time. Most of the time she was bare foot, except now she slid into her heavy socks and cowboy boots. It was chilly outside. She could tell by the moisture that collected on the window when she blew her breath on it. Something Grandpa had taught her. She knew it was cold by feeling the temperature of the glass, but she always blew on it anyway because Grandpa..., she missed him so much. Sigh! Returning to the kitchen, she buttered the toast, poured some coffee, and put on her gloves. Setting her toast on top of the coffee mug she had in one hand, and grabbing the keys with the other, she headed for the front door.

"Ting."

"Oh yes! I almost forgot." Setting her breakfast on the table by the front door, she retrieved the pouch from the bathroom door.

"Sorry about that. Thanks for the reminder."

"Ting!"

After tying the string to the side of her belt, and putting the pouch in her pocket, she picked up her breakfast and headed out the door. Walking across the driveway with the gravel crunching under her boots, she filled her lungs full of cold morning air and almost coughed. *Mmm! It's colder than I thought.* Balancing the toast on top of her coffee, she opened the garage door and got into Grandpa's truck. After she started the engine, she sat there letting it warm up while she ate her toast and sipped coffee. She didn't want cold wet hair all over her shoulders. So without thinking much about it, she parted her hair down the middle and made two braids that hung almost to her waist. She loved this old truck, a 1957 Stepside, Chevy pickup. It was in good condition. Just like Grandpa kept it. She always made sure that it was well maintained. She took it to the car wash in town once a month whether it needed it or not, had it cleaned inside and out, waxed, and polished.

Jerry Flowers, the owner of the car wash, didn't let her forget that he really liked her truck. "If you ever want to sell this beauty, remember I'm the first one you tell. OK?" It became their way to greet one another whenever they saw each other.

"How's my truck runnin'? Giving you any trouble?"

"Still going, Jerry! You'll be the first one on my list to know about any problems."

"You make sure that list only has one person on it."

"And just who might that be?" she teased.

Then he would return with an old English accent. "I haven't the foggiest notion, ma' lady."

"You got it, ma-good man, but don't hold your breath."

Whenever it needed repairs or maintenance, Lilly always rolled up her sleeves and took care of it herself—oil, and filter changes, rotate tires, spark plugs, and any minor jobs. Grandpa and she had worked on it together many times. She learned a lot. Now she called Jerry if the job needed more than one person to do it, like when the transmission needed to be overhauled.

Jerry was always eager to help and would pout if she did too much without his help. "You're going to run me out of business. People around here value your opinion on things. People will think that you don't want me to work on your car. Maybe I'm not good enough." They would both laugh. Jerry Flowers owned the car wash and the gas station next door. He and Lilly had been out to dinner a few times. Nothing serious, "just friends," but Lilly was sure that if she allowed it, things could get serious between them. A woman can tell, but she wasn't up to getting into a relationship any time soon. She respected him for keeping it at "just friends."

He understood, too, that if he got too pushy, she would probably *run* the other way, then he would lose even her friendship, so he just stayed on the sidelines waiting. He was in love with her though, from the first time he saw her. His sister

Summer and she were friends. She had introduced them. It was love at first sight as far as he was concerned. *Someday!* he always told himself. *Someday!* Then he would take a deep breath and just sigh. He was taking her to the Halloween Barn Dance in a week or so. He made sure to ask her as soon as he learned about it. He didn't want to risk someone else asking her first. In fact he drove all the way out to her cabin the day he got up the nerve to ask her. "I was out this way, so I thought I'd stop by and ask . . ."

Smiling at the thought of Jerry's transparent feelings, and drinking the last of her coffee that had already cooled off in the cold air, she put the truck in reverse and backed out of the garage and used the remote control to close the door. She pulled out of the driveway onto the road and turned the radio on. Rock-'n'-roll oldies poured into the cab. She bobbed her head to the music; this always put her in a good mood, but the mood faded when she remembered the concern in Joanne's voice.

In about ten minutes, she pulled into Joanne's driveway. Off to the side was an area big enough to park about five cars, so she parked next to Joanne's car, got out, and walked up the path. Joanne opened the front door before Lilly got to the steps. "Hi!" she said with a quiver in her voice. "Thank you for coming. The longer I think about this, the weirder it seems. I hope I'm not being foolish. Please! Come in. Can I get you some coffee?"

"No thanks. I just finished a cup on the way over. What's up? Are you all right?"

"Yes. Yes, I'm fine," she said, wringing her hands. "Please! Come in the kitchen and I'll show you what I'm talking about."

Lilly followed Joanne into the kitchen.

"Here, please sit at the table, look out the window, and tell me what you see."

"Oh my! Have you started your gardening this early? I would think the ground was too hard to start digging holes."

"I didn't dig that hole. It wasn't there yesterday." "What?" Lilly said, as she stood back up. "Who?"

"I don't know, and I didn't hire anyone to do it either," she said nervously, clearing her throat.

"Have you been out there to see if you can tell what they were digging for?"

"No. Quite frankly it gives me the creeps."

"Wait here. I'll go," Lilly said as she headed for the back door. She closed the door behind her to keep the cold air out of the house.

"Tong."

"Thank you," she whispered and patted the pouch tied to her waistline. "I'll be careful." She went down the back steps; she approached a large hole in the garden. It was a rectangle about seven feet long and almost four feet across, narrowing to about five feet long at the bottom, and almost five feet deep.

"Tong!"

"Yes! I know. This is creepy. It looks like a grave," she said as chills raced up her spine to her neck where the hairs and goose bumps were forming and running down her arms.

"Tong!"

"Yes! This is *not* normal. Something is definitely wrong here." She crossed her arms and shivered, knowing that it wasn't because her hair was still damp. The soil and plants were tossed here and there as if there were no plans of putting them back. At the bottom and around the edges, she found the footprints of at least two different people. One very large boots with heavy tread. The other's average size, looked like tennis shoes. When she turned and walked toward the house, Joanne was standing on the back porch, with her arms folded against the cold air. "I think you had better call the sheriff. This is strange. It appears that someone was looking for something," Lilly said.

"Ting."

"Yes! Come on in out of the cold," Joanne encouraged. "I'll call right now, but what do I say? It sounds kind of silly to complain about somebody digging a hole in my yard."

"Just tell them that your property has been damaged, and you need someone to come out and take a report."

"OK! They would laugh at me if I complained about something like this in the city," she said as she picked up the phone.

"The sheriff is a real nice guy. He'll understand. Besides, it appears that someone was looking for something. They put a lot of time into digging a hole that deep. Especially in this cold weather, the ground is cold and hard. If they didn't find whatever it was, they might be back."

"They must have done it when I was at your house last night. It wasn't there before I left. I was setting here watching some birds use the feeder. I would have seen something that big," she was rambling on nervously and she made herself shut up, *Before this nice young woman could think that I'm a nut. She must think that already.*

"If you would like to make a call, please hang up and try again."

"Oh my!" Joanne was startled by the voice and fluttered with the phone, almost dropping it.

"Here! Let me do that," Lilly said, taking the phone from her friend. She could clearly see that Joanne was more upset than she wanted to show. After she dialed the sheriff's office, she put her free arm around her friend's shoulder reassuringly.

"Sheriff's office. This is Wilson."

"Hi, Don. This is Lilly Patterson."

"Hi there, Lilly! What can it be that brings me the pleasure of your voice, my dear?"

"I'm out here at the old Johnson place with the new owner, Joanne Mason. She's had some vandalism, and I think somebody should check it out."

"Well! Things are slow right now, this will give me something to do. I've been meanin' to head out that way and welcome her to the neighborhood, I can come on out there right now, if she would like."

"Thanks. We'll see you in a few."

"Make that about thirty minutes. One phone call and I'm on my way."

"OK. Thank you. Bye."

Lilly had known Don Wilson, from before he became sheriff. Grandpa used to say, "He's one of the good guys." Don used to be a detective for the sheriff department in Los Angeles, California. There were four deaths in the department in his last year there (one heart and three by gunfire). Much to his wife's relief, he moved her and kids up to the mountains. He was a welcome addition to sheriff's department, was well liked, and was soon unanimously elected sheriff when his boss retired. His two kids are away at college, and up until a year ago, his wife was still with him. She didn't survive the heart attack that took her quickly in the night.

At first he kicked himself for waiting so long to leave the city. Then he learned that it was something that she has had for long time. Never having had much pain with her condition, it went unchecked, and in the middle of the night, her heart just quit working.

TING! THE SILENT WARNING

. . .

As he drove, he thought about the Johnsons. Their kids used to be troublemakers. The oldest one, Gary, was still in jail. Went there right after he beat his wife half to death. He might have killed her, if his dad hadn't showed up to borrow some tools. Ken Johnson knocked his son up side of the head with a chair to get him off of her. Gary hit the floor, knocked out cold. Ken called the paramedics and the sheriff. Don had been to the Johnson place so many times. The youngest boy, Larry, hadn't been in any trouble since his brother was sent away. Got a job, had his own apartment and a girlfriend. Don found himself driving the route absentmindedly, almost as if the patrol car knew where to go all by itself. When he arrived, he parked next to Lilly's truck and got out. Both women were on the porch wearing coats and gloves. They came down the steps to greet the sheriff. "Good morning, ladies. Feels like it could snow soon."

"You're right about that. Don Wilson, this is Joanne Mason. Joanne, this is Don."

"Good morning, Sheriff," Joanne said, smiling nervously. She wasn't used to dealing with the law.

"Please! Call me Don. That sheriff stuff is for out-of-towners," he said and shook her hand. "What can I do for you? Lilly said something about vandalism."

"It's out in the backyard, Sheriff . . . ahh . . . Don. Let me show you, Joanne said as she turned and pointed to show the way.

As they approach the hole, Don said, "Whew! Boy oh boy! Somebody's been busy, haven't they. When did this happen?"

"It wasn't here when I left about five thirty yesterday afternoon. I was at Lilly's until about eight thirty last night, and it was too dark to see anything last night anyway. In fact

I had no reason to even look out here, so I didn't see it until this morning when I was having my coffee at the table. I almost dropped my cup when I saw it. Oh my! I'm babbling, aren't I? I just never expected . . ."

"That's all right. You have good reason to be upset," Lilly said as she put her arm around Joanne's shoulder. "Let's go inside where it's warm. Perhaps Don would like some coffee," she said, looking at him with a wink and pointing her nose in the direction of the house.

"That sounds good to me, Mrs. Mason."

"Please call me Joanne." She blushed.

"OK! Joanne it is. It will be easier to talk inside where it's warm. This hole isn't going anywhere anyway. If it does, I'll have to arrest it."

This brought a smile to Joanne's worried face. "The last person to call me Mrs. Mason was the realtor when she handed me the keys to this place."

"Ladies!" he said as he gestured toward the back door.

. . .

As they drank coffee and ate the pastry Joanne had made that morning (she always cooked when she was nervous), Lilly told her to tell Don about the car.

"What about, what car was that, Joanne?" Don asked. He liked the feel of her name when he said it. *Joanne! If only this wasn't a business call. I'd tell you how pretty you are. But knowing me, I'd lose my nerve.*

Joanne blushed at the look in his eyes and repeated what she had told Lilly on the phone last night and added, "I didn't think anything about it. I assumed that they were lost or something."

"What kind of car was it?"

"I couldn't see very well, no streetlights and all. With my porch light, it appeared to be a dark color. It had, I believe, four doors, not new the shape was wrong. Like one of the old 'gas-hogs' in the sixties or seventies you know, the big boats they made when the size of your car was a status symbol."

"Could you tell how many passengers?"

"When the inside light was on, I saw only one person in the front seat. The back seats are pretty big in those old tubs, and it wasn't lit up like the front. It was dark. I don't know. Maybe it was an old limousine. I'm babbling again. Guess I'm nervous." She smiled then yawned, quickly putting her hand to her face, trying to stop herself.

"This is rather nerve racking, Don. What can we do about this?" Lilly asked.

"Well, to tell the truth, not much right now." His smiled an apology, with both palms facing upward. "But I'm going to ask around. See if anybody has seen a car like you've described. Then go through our vehicle registration files. I know I haven't seen anything like that around here. This is a big area, and not too many folks live here year round. About half in the summer, and half in the winter for the skiing. I'm going to spread the word to some of our locals about your problem. We stick together up here. They'll let me know if they see something unusual, strangers, that old car, or anything else. They always do anyway." He smiled reassuringly and got up from the table. "Please, if you have any more trouble, or even think you do, let me know right away. OK?" Don said, handing her one of his cards, with the office fax and his home telephone numbers on it

"I'll keep in touch with her too, Don. I believe we're becoming good friends."

"Well, Joanne, you couldn't ask for a better friend. This young lady is very capable of taking care of herself and anybody else she decides to take under her wing. She's a lot like her grandfather. He saved my life one time shortly after I got here. Long story . . . maybe another time."

"I'd like to hear it sometime. Seriously! I thought I'd be all right up here by myself. I'm starting to wonder. I'm feeling a little foolish. After all, it's only a hole. Maybe they got what they came for and this is the end of it."

"Better safe than sorry," Lilly said. "We don't know that for sure. Why don't you stay at my house a few days and let Don figure this out?"

"No," Joanne said. "I've already put you to too much of a bother. Nobody's going to keep me away from my own home. I'm not giving in to fear."

"Tong."

"Lilly's right. It wouldn't hurt to be cautious," Don encouraged. "Why don't you go to her place for at least one night. I'll find out what the folks around here have seen by tomorrow. Then we will know where we stand on this. If they didn't find what they were looking for, they might come back. No telling what they might do if they don't find whatever it is. As a matter of fact, if you don't mind, I'd like to be here tonight just in case. I'll keep the lights off to make it look like you're not home. Maybe they'll show, and we can put an end to this mischief before the night is over."

"I don't know," Joanne pondered.

"Come on, Joanne! What else have you got to do? A sleepover, you'll be the first person I've had over night in a long time. Please?! It'll be fun. Say yes, pleeeease," she mock whined.

"Well! . . . OK! If you think it's best. It could be fun," she gave in. "I'll get a change of clothes, my jammys, and my toothbrush. I'll be over at your place before dark. I really do appreciate your concern, both of you."

"Ting."

"I'm going to have my deputy bring me over there to get your key to the house and drop me off over here. It won't do any good if there's a police car parked outside. How about I come over to Lilly's place about four o'clock."

"Yah! It gets dark early this time of year," Lilly added.

"Well! . . . OK. I'll be there about four then, Joanne confirmed.

Don headed for the front door. "I'm going to make my rounds and see what I can find out before then. I'll show myself out. See you ladies later."

"Good bye, Don, and thank you."

"Bye! See you later," Lilly added, and when he shut the door, "Grandpa was right. He is one of the good guys. He'll get to the bottom of this. Don't you worry."

"Won't his wife worry about him being out all night at somebody else's house? A good-looking man like that might need some watching."

"He's widowed."

"Oh my! I'm sorry. I didn't mean . . ."

"That's OK. Stop blushing. I think you two would make a cute couple," Lilly teased.

Joanne's face turned another shade darker. "Oh dear."

Lilly gave her a big smile and pointed at her with her eyebrows. "Well!

You would."

. . .

Don, too, had a smile on his face as he started back to the office. *A fine-looking lady there. Poor thing is scared and afraid to show it. She's trying to be brave.* As he drove, the smile became sour just thinking about the Johnson kids. *If they do anything to hurt her . . . I'll bet they're back to get something they left behind. They just couldn't get it while the folks were still there. Last I heard the oldest boy, Gary Johnson, was in jail. I know that Larry Johnson wouldn't try anything like this by himself. Must be something of value for them to go to all this trouble. I wouldn't put it past them, to cause Joanne trouble if they don't get what they're looking for.* He wanted to check the status of Gary's jail sentence. He called the office on his radio, telling John to get a request for information faxed to the Bureau of Corrections, ASAP (as soon as possible).

. . .

CHAPTER 4

Becka Freeman was rubbing her cheek. She hadn't felt his hand across her face in three years. "Gary! Stop it. I'm not your wife anymore," she yelled, trying to pull away from his grip on her wrist. Gary had strong-armed his way into her cottage. "I'm married now, and Tom is due home anytime."

"Yeah! Like I'm real scared. Shakin' in my boots," he sneered and released her arm.

"You'd better be gone when he gets here," she warned.

"You won't be married when I get through with him. You're mine. Don't you remember? 'Til death do we part?"

"Death is right, you killed our marriage with your anger and violence. You were served with divorce papers in jail," she reminded him.

"That don't mean shit to me. You're mine!" he screamed, spraying spit in her face, as he towered over her five foot, five inches with his six foot, three inches and two hundred sixty pounds.

"It's too late, Gary, I'm pregnant. I'm in love with Tom, and he's good to me. He doesn't beat me, like you used to. I can see what you are now. How could have I been so dumb to believe that you loved me? You just wanted to own me. Tell me what to do and have me wait on you. You're the big bully from school that never grew up." She knew that she shouldn't be speaking to him this way, but it felt good to be telling him to back off. Being naive enough to think that the divorce papers would be enough to hold him off, she continued. "After you sent me to the hospital, where I almost died by the way," she said with her hands on her hips, "I knew that you couldn't really love me. So I filed for divorce right after I got out and was able to drive to my lawyer's office. I'm not about to spend any more time with you. So just leave."

"It's not that easy, baby. We are joined in the eyes of God. 'Let no man come between us'!" he yelled.

"And God knows that you're the one that pulled us apart. You did it with your anger and your fists. You'd better leave. Tom's pulling into the driveway right now," she said, looking out the front window, when she heard the gravel crunching in the driveway.

Gary spun around to look out the window. "You haven't seen the last of me." He grabbed her by the forearms, squeezing hard, lifting her off the floor, and shook her above his head.

"Tommy, help me!" she screamed.

She fell to the floor after he threw her against the wall. He looked out the window again and saw Tom running toward the front door. Turning around, he ran for the back door, disappearing into the woods behind the house.

Becka was on the kitchen floor when Tom rushed in. She was sitting up, leaning against the cabinet, holding her stomach with one hand and her head with the other. "Becka!"

He went to his knees beside her. "Oh dear God! Sweetheart, what's happening here?" he asked, pulling her into his arms.

"Gary was here. He forced his way into the house. He hurt me. My stomach hurts," she said, trying unsuccessfully to hold the tears back, and melted into his arms.

"Stay right here." Tom went into the bathroom and brought back a wet wash cloth and gave it to Becka for her face. "That SOB, I'm calling the sheriff right after I call an ambulance," Tom said as he picked her up and carried her into the bedroom. "Looks like he roughed you up pretty bad. Where does it hurt, sweetheart? I need to know what to tell the medics when they get here."

"Stomach, neck, my back, everything." Then she broke down and cried.

"This is Thomas Freeman. We need an ambulance right away. My wife has been beaten up by her ex-husband, and she's pregnant . . . five and a half months . . . Hurry! Please! She's in bad shape." He gave the directions and address, hung up the wall phone, and checked on Becka before he called the sheriff's office.

"Sheriff's office. This is Deputy Cameron."

"John, this is Tom Freeman. Is the sheriff in?"

"Not right now, he's out on a call. Can I help you?

"Becka's ex-husband was just here. He hurt her pretty bad. I've already called an ambulance."

"I'm getting on the radio as we speak. Hold on a minute."

"OK . . . I thought that SOB was in jail," he said angrily.

"To my knowledge, I thought he was too. Hold on, he's responding."

"Sheriff! This is John. We've got trouble out at the Freeman place. Her ex just beat her up. The medics are on their way out there right now. Out."

"Thanks, John. I'm right down the road from there. Tell them I'll be there in about ten minutes. Over and out."

John got back on the telephone. "Don's on his way. Should get there in about ten minutes."

"Thanks, John. I'll talk to you later. Bye."

"OK! Later, Tom."

. . .

Don reached over and turned the emergency lights on and then the siren. As he sped toward the Freeman place, he got back on the radio and told John to get hold of the prison and put a rush on that status report. "We need to find out as soon as possible about Gary Johnson's prison sentence. Call me the minute the report comes in. After you finish that, go over to the old Johnson place and talk to the new owner, Joanne Mason. Make some plaster casts of the footprints and a soil sample out in her backyard. Looks like the boys have been lookin' for something they left behind. Somebody dug a big-assed hole in her garden. Over."

"You sure it was them? Over."

"That's what we're going to find out. Get the job done before dark and get back to the office. I'm going to need you later. Over."

"Yes, sir. Over and out."

"Damn kids! Still makin' trouble. They've gone too far this time," he said aloud.

. . .

Tom was holding the door open when the ambulance arrived. He waited for them to get the stretcher out of the back of the vehicle. As they approached, he told them, "She's in the bedroom to your right." Before he could close the door, the sheriff pulled into the driveway and rushed into the house.

"Don, I'm glad you're here. Thank you for coming so soon."

"I wasn't far from here. How is she? I need to talk to her if she can."

Tom closed the door and showed the sheriff to the bedroom. As they entered the room, they saw her being hooked up to a heart monitor, and a blood pressure cuff was around her arm. One of the paramedics was listening to her abdomen for signs that the baby might be in distress. The other one was transmitting her EKG results to the hospital and talking on the radio.

"We need to take her in to be checked out by the doctor. I believe she's going to be all right. The baby seems to be OK too, but we want to be sure. We'll have the doctor confirm it."

"Tommy! I don't want to go to the hospital. I feel fine, just a little sore," Becka complained.

"I know you don't, sweetheart, but let's have the baby checked out. OK?" Tom said.

"Yes, you're right, of course," she agreed.

"Why don't you stay and talk to the sheriff before you follow us in?" the paramedic encouraged.

"They're probably going to take some tests, and it will be a while before they let her go."

"OK, sweety. I'll be there shortly," Tom said, bending down to kiss her forehead. "Don wants to have a word with you before you leave, if you're up to it."

"OK, honey," she said, turning her head to face Don. "Not as bad as last time, huh? At least I can talk this time. What can I tell you besides the fact that it was Gary?"

"Do you know why he came here?"

"Just to make trouble. He said that I wouldn't be married to Tom anymore after he got through with him." This brought tears to her eyes, but she continued. Proudly putting her chin in the air, she said, "He doesn't know who he's messing with. My Tom here is an expert and an instructor of martial arts. He'll kick his ass if he gets hold of him. In fact when I told him that Tom was coming up the driveway, he picked me up, shook me, then he threw me against the wall, then ran like a chicken out the back door. He's not very brave, but he is out of his mind crazy. The look in his eyes! They were strange, and full of evil. I wouldn't put anything past him. He's dangerous. I've seen that look before."

"Can you tell me what he was wearing?" Don asked, patting her on the shoulder to calm her down, if that was possible.

"Well he had on the same thing he always wears. Blue denim jeans, Lumberjack boots, red and green plaid shirt, a dark blue baseball cap with a big A on it for the Angels. Oh yeah! A black nylon ski jacket. It looked new, the kind that hangs down to your thighs," she said excitedly. At this point, she rubbed her stomach and groaned.

"We'd better get going, sir," one of the paramedics said as they lifted her onto the stretcher.

Don said, "Let's go in the other room for a minute. Let them get her packed up for the trip."

"I'll just be in the other room for a minute, honey."

"Where was she when you came home?" Don asked as they left the room.

"In the kitchen on the floor. Here I'll show you." He gestured toward the other room. "It scared me to death, and my heart skipped a couple of beats when I first saw her down there. I thought she had gone into early labor until I got a good look at her. Then she told me it was Gary. That bastard had better not let me see him first."

"I know you're upset, but if you find him, tell me first. We'll both go get him, and then it will be legal. We don't need you behind bars for taking the law into your own hands." Don was looking into Tom's eye. "Promise me, Tom. You need to be here for Becka and the baby. Promise!"

It took Tom about thirty seconds before he relented. "OK. I know you're right. It's just that I'm so *angry.*"

"If you want to talk some of that anger off, just get in touch with me. OK?"

"Yes, I understand. I will."

"Ahh! Excuse me? Do you have a pair of work boots, or hiking boots?"

"No, not work boots, but we both have walking shoes. Why do you ask?" "Look at these little chunks of dirt on the floor here," Don said, pointing.

They both knelt down to get a closer look. "These look like they came from the tread of a large boot."

"Yeah! Like the ones that I've seen the highway workers wearing. The light tannish orange ones," Tom said as though he had a picture of them in his mind. "As a matter of fact," Tom said, looking around on the floor, "there's a trail of them all the way from the front door. I'll bet they're Gary's."

"Yep! I believe you're right on that one. Lumberjack boots are close to the same thing. Don't clean anything up yet. I'll have some lab boys come out from the city. Take some pictures and prints. At least we'll be able to prove he was here and send his butt back to jail."

"I thought he *was* in jail?" Tom asked with anger. "For another three years anyway. Did he break out or something?"

"I'm having that checked out as we speak. I should know soon enough."

"Mr. Freeman, we'll be taking her in now," said the young paramedic standing in the kitchen doorway.

"Oh. Yeah!" Tom was brought back to the moment.

"I'll walk you out. Excuse me, Sheriff."

"No problem! I'll wait here," Don informed him.

As they took the stretcher outside, Tom asked, "How are you feeling, honey?"

"Mmm! Sal-right," she slurred.

"We gave her something to relax her. Don't worry, it won't harm the baby. I think she'll be all right. She's upset and bruised up some. The doctor will check them both over real good when we get there," the young man said reassuringly.

"I'll be there shortly. I just need to finish up with the sheriff first," he said and then kissed his wife before they lifted her into the back of the ambulance. "I won't be long, honey."

"Mmm-kay! Love you."

"Love you too, sweety!" He watched until their tail lights disappeared and then returned to the house. "You find anything else?"

"Not really. He wasn't here very long. Maybe some prints on the table and the back door. Remember don't clean anything until the other guys finish. I'm going to try to get them here by tomorrow morning, at the latest. It might be too late for them to come out this far tonight. It's an hour's drive from headquarters downtown," Don informed him.

"OK! Then if you're finished, I'd like to get going."

"If you two can think of anything else, let me know," Don said, handing him a card with the office, fax, and his home telephone numbers on it. "Try not to walk on the floor where the dirt is. We might get a whole shoe print out of that one by the sink. I took a couple pictures while you were outside, but the lab guys like to do their own thing with them. We'll see you later."

"Bye, Don, and thanks again," Tom said, shutting the front door. He leaned against the door and tried to calm his own nerves down some before driving to the hospital. He closed his eyes and did some of the deep breathing exercises that he taught in martial arts class. After about a minute, he bent over, touched his toes, and just hung there for a few seconds. Standing up, he went around the house to check all the locks, and then left the house.

. . .

It was three forty-five when Joanne pulled into the driveway. She took her small overnight bag out of the back seat and locked the door. She stood there admiring the cabin. Lilly had dressed it up real nice. All of the windowframes were painted white and the shutters were of natural weathered wood the same as the log cabin was built of. It had a big wide front porch and roof the full width of the cabin. The hand rails and posts were painted white to match the windows, the rest was weather-worn wood that also matched the cabin. Along the path leading to the front door were logs about two feet around and various lengths. The shortest being one and a half foot, and the tallest at about a two and a half foot long. These were stacked on end, one next to the other forming a line along each side of the path. On top of each one, Lilly had made large music notes so that when you see it from a side view, it looked like maybe it was a song that had been written. She looked toward the sound of someone tapping on a window. She could see Lilly in the kitchen window, waving at her to come on in.

Putting her bags down inside by the door, she went to see what Lilly was doing. "Hey, kiddo, I made it. I was just admiring your home. Now that I've seen it in daylight, I really like what you've done with the logs next to the path."

"Thanks! I talked Grandpa into doing that when I was a teenager. He had just cut a tree down, those logs were supposed to be firewood. When the snow gets deep, it makes it easier to get a direct line to the house. It's just wide enough for the snow blower too. Clears the path in one pass."

"He must have loved you very much. Sounds like you had a good relationship."

"Yes, we did, and I miss him like crazy."

"Ting."

"I'm just starting dinner. You owe me big time now. Two in a row," she teased and laughed. "Just kidding! I enjoy your company." She smiled.

With a smile of her own, Joanne said, "Don't worry, dear, I'll make it up to you, so well that you'll end up owing me. 'Nuff said. OK? Now I need to start working off part of my debt." Without another word, Joanne started washing the utensils and bowls that had been used to prepare dinner. Then she set the table for the two of them. "The sheriff's here," she said, looking out the window. "He looks different in regular clothes, even better than his uniform." She dried her hands and went to get the keys out of her purse.

Lilly answered the door. "Hi, Don! Come on in."

"No thanks, I should get over there and settle in before dark."

"Hello, Sheriff," Joanne said. "Here's the keys."

"Thanks! I'll be careful not to disturb anything."

"I'm not worried. Lilly says you're an honest man. Just be careful. I'd hate to think that you might get hurt if they come back."

"They'd better look out for Don. He's a tough guy," Lilly added.

"If you get hungry, there's lots of food in the refrigerator. Help yourself to whatever's in there. Just pop it in the microwave."

"No, that's fine. I brought something with me for supper."

"I always make too much of everything. It's hard to cook for just one person, after feeding a family for so many years." *Oh dear, I hope he doesn't think I'm throwing myself at him,* she thought to herself and blushed.

"If that pastry this morning is an example of your cooking, I'd better not."

"Sheriff!" Lilly chastised.

"No! I meant that if everything tastes *as good,* I'll have trouble staying awake. Food does that to me. Nothing like a little nap after a good meal. I need to be alert, is what I meant to say," he said with his own pink cheeks.

Smiling, Joanne said, "There's a fresh pot of coffee in the pot by the sink."

"Thanks! I know, I could use some of that. I'm going to be awake all night. I'll call over here if anything happens tonight. Otherwise, I'll see you ladies in the morning. Good evening," he said, tipping the brim of his cap before returning to the patrol car.

"Are you blushing, boss?" John asked with a big smile.

"Maybe you should ask her to the Halloween Barn Dance. It's next weekend, remember?"

This made him blush even more so. John and he had been friends for about seven years, and they knew each other very well. John and his wife had followed Don up here from Los Angeles. One visit with Don and Sally was all it took to convince them to move here. They had backed each other up in a few bad situations over the years and would trust each other with their own lives. Both John and Laura Cameron had been there for him when his wife, Sally, passed away. Don felt that John was the brother that he had never had. They talked about everything together. "She is a nice-looking lady, isn't she? Well, that's beside the point. I don't want to be too forward, I just met her. I could invite her as a way to get acquainted with her new neighbors," Don said thoughtfully.

"Now that sounds like a plan," his friend said, as he stopped in front of Joanne's driveway. "If you need help, just buzz me at home. I can be here in less than fifteen minutes. OK?"

"Yah! See ya later."

Don waited for him to pull away before walking up to the house. Before he went inside, he checked the damage in the backyard. He wanted to make sure that there wasn't any plaster traces left around the impressions that John had made earlier. *Nope! It looks like it did when I left. John does good work. We don't want Gary knowing we've been here.* After that, he walked the parameter of the property. He needed to become familiar with all the surroundings. He found what appeared to be a well-worn path in the north corner that was lined with small pebbles. They were probably to keep your shoes out of the mud when it rains. The trail led off into the woods. He went through the opening and picked up a small piece of deadwood (that's a branch that sometimes naturally falls off of a tree) and broke off a small piece and stuck it loosely in the ground on the small path leading into the yard. After rummaging through Joanne's trash barrel, he came up with a couple empty cans. These, he balanced on the small branch. Someone could approach the backyard without coming in through the front of the property. If they did, Don would hear the cans falling on the small rocks when the branch was disturbed. Gary would know about the trail, because he used to live here with his brother and parents. So he knew this whole property very well. Don finished looking around and went into the house through the back door.

There was still enough light to see fairly well without turning any lights on. He went into each room and looked out the windows, leaving the blinds open just enough to see outside, and still look like nobody was home. He went back into the kitchen and settled down at the table with a cup of coffee. The DMV and the state prison had faxed reports that came in just before they were leaving the office. He had brought them with him and was now going through the papers.

According to these reports, Gary Manfred Johnson was released early, with good behavior. Because of the overcrowding in the prison system, this was being done frequently. That's all we need. Well! When we catch him, he's going right back where he belongs. Destruction of private property, assault and battery, and whatever else he's doing when we catch him. Neither one of those boys have been any good, but Gary's the worst. Larry Johnson, his brother, is just his dedicated follower. He hasn't been any trouble since Gary was put away. Now Gary's back and the trouble starts again.

"Wreeeak!" That sounds like brakes. Don ran to the front door and looked through the curtains. There was a big old Cadillac, Fleetwood stopped in front of the house. That's probably the car that Joanne saw last night. There were two people in the front seat. Men, one large and one smaller. Odds are we know who you are, Don thought to himself. After it drove away, he went into the kitchen to check the DMV report of cars ten years or older, registered in Oregon. It was a large document, but with what he had just seen, it was going to be much easier. The list was conveniently organized by year, model, and registered owner. The car he had just seen was at least a 1960 something. That would make it thirty or forty years old. He ran his finger down the list of about two hundred seventy-five 1960s vehicles and marked the Cadillacs. After he finished that, he went back over the list and found seven registered in this part of the state. He found it! There it is, a 1965 Cadillac license number "65 CADDY" registered to a Donna Maxwell. He went to the phone and called information. After he got the phone number, he called Donna Maxwell.

"Hello?"

"This is Sheriff Wilson with the sheriff's department. I'm trying to reach a Donna Maxwell."

"This is Donna. How can I help you?"

"I'm calling about your 1965 Cadillac."

"If this about the ad in the paper, you're too late. I just sold it to a young man last week," she said as if she was truly sorry.

"Do you have his name?" he asked.

"Yes! I'll never forget it either," she said angrily.

Detecting the strain in her voice, he asked, "Is there a problem?"

"Well, he seemed like such a nice young fellow. His name is Larry Johnson. There was another older guy with him. When the car was paid for, this older guy grabs the keys and insists on driving."

"Did you get the other fellow's name?" Don inquired.

"I think he called him Perry, or Gary . . . something like that," she recalled. "Well! I'll tell you one thing, he was a big bully. He was big and he kind of scared me. That poor kid. He pushed Larry right out of the way and got in the driver's seat. The car was parked on the front lawn, and when he left, he spun the tires and dug up the lawn all the way out to the street and over the curb. I told Larry that he needed to take good care of it, because it's an old car. I only charged him three hundred dollars for it 'cause it needs some work done on it. If that other fellow keeps driving like that, it won't last very long at all. That's about all I can tell you. I hope I've been some help," she said with her nervous, old lady voice.

"Yes, you have, Mrs. Maxwell. Thank you very much. Just tell me one more thing if you can. Please."

"Yes, of course. what might that be?"

"What color is the car?"

"Navy blue. Is there anything else?"

"No. Thank you very much! You have made my job much easier. Thanks again."

"Well! That's good. I hope everything turns out OK. Larry seemed like such a nice young man. I hope he's not in trouble. He needs to get away from that other guy. That one just *looks* like trouble. Call back if you need to."

"Yes! And thanks again. Bye," he said and hung up the phone, and then called John at home.

"Cameron residence," the voice of John's eleven-year-old daughter Tammy, always put a smile on Don's face.

"This is Uncle Don, sweetheart. Is your daddy home?"

"Yes, he is, but I want to ask you something first. OK?"

"OK. What is it, baby?"

"Are you still going to take Junior and I shopping for Mommy's birthday present?"

"Of course, we have a date, remember?"

"So what time are you picking us up?" she asked and then giggled. She loved surprises. They had been saving their allowances for this.

"Why don't we figure that out later. Her birthday isn't until the week before Thanksgiving."

"OK! Here's Daddy. Bye, Uncle Don. I love you."

"Love you too, baby, bye!"

"Yeah! What's up, Don?" John asked.

"I've been looking through this paperwork. Gary's our guy, all right." Then he told him about the early release and the conversation he just had with Mrs. Maxwell about the car. "They were stopped in front of the house a few minutes ago."

"That's bold of them. You need me over there?"

"The less traffic in and out of here, the better. I'll call you the minute they show up. Notify the office and have them be on standby. Let's see who's on duty tonight?"

"Bill Thompson and Sara Forester. I'll call and fill them in on what's going on."

"They already know I'm over here, but fill them in on what I just told you."

"Will do. Anything else?"

"Not right now. Talk to you later."

"OK! I'll be by the phone. Bye."

"Bye." Don hung up the telephone and opened the refrigerator. Inside was a blue light instead of white. "Now that's pleasant. No bright light glaring in your eyes in the middle of the night. A woman after my own heart. Look out, Don. You're talking to yourself," he chided himself. He couldn't stop thinking about the new woman. Being in her home all night wasn't helping.

CHAPTER 5

"It looks like she's not home again, Gary. What you want'a do now? Maybe we should wait until after it gets darker. I don't want to park in the driveway either. This makes me real nervous. What if she comes home while we're there?"

"Don't worry about it!" Gary yelled at his brother. "Will you just shut up?

You talk too much! Hasn't anybody ever told you that?"

"I'm sorry. I get talkative when I'm nervous."

Gary sat in the passenger seat looking at the house. "Dad and Mom were supposed to give us this place, or we wouldn't be going through all this trouble," Gary sneered. "Damn," he said and slammed his fist against the dashboard.

"They decided to sell it after you went to jail. They spent a fortune on lawyers. They didn't have any money left in their savings."

"If they only knew about the bank money I buried, they wouldn't be so anxious to leave this place," Gary said.

"*Bank* money? I saw the money we got last night, but you didn't say we were digging for *bank* money. When did you do that?"

"A couple guys I know did it with me. Before I went to jail for hittin' Becka. The police still don't know who did it. We split the money and went our separate ways. It was so cool."

"So how much was your share? What bank did you rob?"

"Not a bank. A bank truck. You know, one of those armored trucks."

"WOW! Where was this at?"

"Up on one of the mountain roads in the middle of the night. One of the guys I did the job with used to work for the armored truck company. He was the driver on a special night delivery. He stopped the truck and held a gun to the other guy's head until the two guys in the back opened up. Then we made them load the money into the van we were driving."

"Won't they be able to tell the cops who did it? I mean, they worked together."

"They won't be telling anybody, anything." "

You mean you? You didn't kill them, did you?"

"Yep! Just like it was nothing," Gary bragged. "We each did one of the other guys. That way nobody could point any fingers," Gary continued bragging as he took a drag on his cigarette and blew several smoke rings.

"Well, how much did you get?" Larry asked again.

Inhaling smoke from his mouth into his nose, he held his breath and said, "More than enough, little brother. The less you know, the better." Exhale. "If we play our cards right, we won't be working for a living ever again."

"Let's get something to eat, I'm starved."

"Sounds like a plan, good buddy. Get this bucket of bolts movin'."

. . .

Lilly and Joanne finished the dinner dishes and were sitting in the front room, enjoying a cup of tea in front of the fireplace. "This is really nice," Joanne said. "Thank you for being my friend."

"You're easy to like. I believe that the good Lord puts people where they are supposed to be. It's up to them how they handle the situation. We were supposed to meet the other night, and I'm supposed to help you. It just feels like the right thing to do."

"Ting."

"You have a wonderful attitude toward life. I hope that some of it rubs off on me. I didn't have any idea which way my life was heading when I moved up here. All I knew was that, like you said, 'It just felt right,' to be getting away from the life I had. It was a dead end."

"What made you want to move from the city all the way up here in the mountains?"

"That's the strangest thing too. A friend of mine introduced me to her friend that was in real estate. After we talked a while, she showed me some pictures of smaller houses that I could move into. Moving seemed like a good idea. It would get me away from that big old house that I was living in by myself. The worse part was when I would walk from room to empty room. It made being alone almost unbearable. All the reminders day after day. I cried so much there weren't any more tears left."

"That sounds dreadful. You *poor* dear."

"We even looked at a few of the houses. Once I was inside of these houses, I just couldn't see myself living in any of them. One day we were sitting in a restaurant having brunch waiting for an appointment to see yet *another* house. One of her picture books fell on the floor when she was trying to move it out of the way for the waitress who had brought our food. The waitress picked it up for her. When she held it out for her to take, the picture of my new house fell out. It landed on the table right in front of me. 'This is a sign,' I told myself. I picked it up, looked at it, and liked it right off. I asked her if I could see this one, and she said, 'It's all the way up in the mountains, was I really sure that I would want to move that far away from everything?' Just holding the picture in my hand, it felt right. We made arrangements to come up here and look at it."

"Well! I'm glad you did."

"The minute I walked into the house, I knew that I was going to take it. Something inside me just got all warm and cozy feeling. It feels good to be here. My friends at work, *and* my kids tried to talk me out of it. I was hearing none of it though. I told them, 'This is my life and I'm going to try it. If I fail at living in the mountains, then I could always move back to the city.' And, 'No! I won't mind moving again if that's the way things turn out. I had to find out for myself.' That's the only way to know for sure. If I didn't try, there would always be a doubt in the back of my mind."

"How do you feel about it now?" Lilly asked.

"I'm not going anywhere. My roots have already started to take hold," Joanne said with a big smile.

"This trouble you're having won't last long. It's usually pretty peaceful around here," Lilly informed her.

"I'm sure it can't be as bad as where I was living. All the gangs, drive-by shootings, people going crazy, and it costs more to live there too. I never want to live in the city again."

"Are you going to stay retired, or would you like to find a job?"

"If retirement means sitting around with nothing to do. Hmm! I don't know if I could. I've got to keep busy. If I keep cooking like I have been, I'll end up being as big as a house."

"Didn't you say that you had a dressmaking shop of your own?"

"Yes, I had a shop and three ladies working for me. Business was good. One of the ladies bought the business from me when I told her that I was closing up shop. I wonder if there's much of a call for that around here?"

"There's always a need for clothes to be made. There are a lot of people with money around here. I'm sure that if the word got around, you'd have more than enough to keep you busy. What kind of clothing did you make?"

"We did everything from baby clothes to wedding dresses, formal gowns, and men's clothes too. We even got a contract with the local theater to make their costumes. One of my specialties was clothing for larger-sized people. It's really hard to buy anything off the rack that looks good on big people. One of my customers said that he wanted me to continue making things for him by mail. I just received an order from him yesterday. I brought four different kinds of sewing machines with me. I could look into it."

"Well see? There ya go. We could make up some fliers and mail them to everybody. I'm sure that we could get a list of addresses around here from the post office. Let me know when you're ready and we'll do it," Lilly said excitedly.

"This is sure a turn of events. I was wondering what I was going to do with myself. I like the idea."

"Anything I can do to help, just let me know."

"Ring! Ring!"

"Excuse me a minute," Lilly said, and then answered the phone.

. . .

Later that evening, the two brothers were parked on a narrow dirt road in the woods. The plants had taken over because nobody had used this road since they were out here last time. It was a place that they had often gone as kids. About fifteen feet up, in a large walnut tree, was the tree fort that they had built years ago when they wanted to get away from the folks. Their folks didn't come out here. The boys never told them about it. It was about three hundred yards from their old backyard. It was still in pretty good shape, but somehow it seemed smaller than they remembered. They still had room for both to lay down on the floor, without knocking the two chairs and a table over. "Get the ice chest out of the trunk. I'm going on up and you can hand it up to me," Gary ordered.

This was where Gary had been staying since he'd gotten out of jail. He had a small portable television, sleeping bags, blankets, five-gallon bottles of water, some utensils, and a couple packages of paper plates and cups. In the corner was a trash bag full of empty takeout food containers. "You outta get that trash out of here, it's growin' bugs."

"Get it out your own self," Gary barked.

"It's not my mess!" Larry retorted.

"Then don't complain. We'll take it with us when we leave."

Without another word, Larry tied the trash bag closed and dropped it out the door onto the ground below. I'm always cleanin' up your messes, he thought to himself. I wish you'd never come back. I was gettin' along just fine without you. You didn't learn anything in jail, did you? I'm not tellin' you about my job or my girlfriend either.

When Gary called to say that he was out of jail on good behavior, Larry panicked. He never talked about Gary to anyone that he met since his brother had gone to jail. He was trying to get his life together and be a good person. He had a good job at the hardware store and was starting to feel like a regular person again. He had worked there almost three years, and his boss told him that he was getting a bonus this

Christmas, because he had done such a good job. He didn't want his big brother screwing things up for him. He told his boss that he had important family business that couldn't wait and took two weeks' emergency leave. He told his girlfriend almost the same thing. He got along with Danny Lovett (his boss) very well. In fact, Danny, the owner, had invited Larry and Susan over to dinner with the family several times in these last three years. Danny's brother Howard Lovett was always finding small jobs for him to do. Mostly carpentry. Larry was very good with his hands. As the word spread in the small community, Larry always had small jobs to do. He met Susan at one of those jobs. She kept calling for him to help her with things until he got the nerve to ask her out. The rest was history. If he told Gary about his new life, or Susan, he knew that Gary would do *something* to mess things up for him. Besides he didn't like the way that Gary treated women. Poor Becka, she's a real nice girl, that had a lot going for her until Gary came along. *How come the good ones always end up with the bad ones?* he wondered.

Then there were the beatings. He almost killed Becka. He had gone to see Becka in the hospital and been to her house a few times in the last few months. Her new husband is a really nice guy. Tom gave him some pointers on self-defense. He was real happy for her when she met and married Tom Freeman. He even went to their wedding. He couldn't understand how a person could hurt someone they loved. Larry didn't know about the latest trouble that Gary had started with the ex-wife. Larry told himself that he would help his brother until he found whatever it was that Gary was looking for, and that would be it. Then Gary was on his own. Now that he knew about the robbery and murder, he was scared that everything would fall apart. He had to figure a way to get away from his brother. But how? He would have to bide his time and think of something.

He couldn't run; Gary would find him and probably kill him too now that he knew about the robbery and all. *Oh God! Why did he have to tell me all that stuff? How am I going to get out of this? Lord, help me! Please!*

"We'll leave as soon as this TV program is over," Gary said. "That should be long enough for it to get dark outside."

CHAPTER 6

"Tinkle! . . . Clang!"

"What the . . . That stupid old broad. She thinks this will keep out the trespassers. Well it ain't going to do you any good if you're not home," Gary mocked childishly, his chin sticking out in the direction of the house.

While they were in the tree house, Gary told Larry that he had buried most of his stash next to the house. Their dad was repairing the back porch. It was the kind that was raised up off the ground, with a crawl space under it. Gary offered to do it for him, and this gave him the opportunity to put his money where nobody would find it by accident. He crawled underneath and dug a hole and buried the larger part of the money and then finished the porch. The one that he dug up in the garden last night was still in the plastic bags that he had wrapped it in, but some of the money was ruined. It was moldy and part of it tore when they tried to separate the bills. He was worried about the money under the porch too, but the rain and snow couldn't get at it under there. So it should in better condition.

. . .

Don heard the cans fall and went to look out the window in the bedroom. The cans had done their job. Both of the Johnson boys were in the backyard. Gary was telling his brother. "Come on! Hurry up. What are you afraid of? She's not home."

Don picked up the telephone next to the bed and called John. "They're here. Call the office and get the other deputies over here. I'm going to stay inside to see what they're up to."

"Bang! Bang! Bang."

"Sounds like they're knocking on the back door. Get over here," he said and hung up the phone. He was hoping that they weren't planning on coming into the house. Don quietly eased his way to the back door. *Are they knocking on the door?* When he looked, there was nobody standing there. *Guess not.*

Bang! Bang! Creak.

It sounded like a nail being pulled out of wood. Don looked out another window and could make out two figures working on something at the side of the back porch. It sounded like they were tearing a whole in the house, or the porch. *I'm glad Joanne's not here. This would have scared her something awful. My men should be here shortly. I hope they don't do too much damage before that.*

"Looks like the old man didn't like the job I did. He's got some extra nails in here. Damn! I hope he didn't find it."

"Don't tear the place apart. Remember, it doesn't belong to us anymore," Larry reminded him.

"Would you shut up and get down here and help me. Hold the light over here. No! Right there, stupid. Now hold it still, you're shakin' it all over the place. Hand me the pliers, maybe I can pull this nail out."

"I don't know why you're getting mad at me. I didn't put anything under there. Fact is I don't even want any of your bank money. I didn't take or bury it. And I didn't kill anybody to get it."

Gary stood up and looked down at his brother. "What are you saying?"

"That it's not mine. I didn't earn it, and I didn't do anything to keep it."

"Well, little brother. I did it for us. Don't you know that?"

"Yes, but those guys had to die for it. That's not right."

"What are you, a goody-two-shoes now? What were we supposed to do? Leave them there tied up so that they could tell everybody about it later? Use your head." Gary's voice was raised to a higher pitch. "The way it is now, the cops don't know jack shit about anything. They're still scratching their heads on this one. Unless you say something, nobody's going to know anything."

Larry came back at him with his own anger. He couldn't help himself. "I didn't ask you to do this. I don't want your money. I've got a good job, and I make fairly good money of my own."

Then he fell to the ground as Gary punched him in the jaw. Boom! Down! "Shut up and help me."

At this point, Don drew his gun. He was prepared to shoot Gary right through the window. He understood the relationship now. Larry was just the gofer being bullied by his bigger, older brother. When he tries to stand up to him, Gary just punches him out.

Larry just laid there, out of self-defense. Every time in the past that he had gotten back up, he got slugged again, even harder. He lay there rubbing his face.

"Get up!" Gary yelled. "You'll help me with this damn thing, if you know what's good for you. Now that you know about it, you're just as guilty as I am. So shut up your yapping and get to work."

Larry turned over on his hands and knees pushing himself up. "You haven't changed one bit after bein' in jail. I thought you were supposed to learn not to be violent anymore."

"Just the opposite, little brother. Ya gotta be tough to survive in there. A guy like you would be somebody's sweetheart in no time. They'd like those tight little buns of yours. There's no such thing as a virgin in the big house, so keep your lip shut and we'll do just fine. There's nobody knows about this but us."

"You told me that the other guys went their separate ways."

"What? You think I'm nuts? I ain't going to leave nobody around that can rat on me," Gary bragged. "Besides, after the first guy, the rest were easy, and I got all the money. Don't forget. I did it for us. You can forget that puny little job of yours now. We're rich, do you understand that? We are rich. Now shut up, and give me a hand here."

Don was cursing himself for not bringing his tape recorder. *If I can get Larry away from his brother and explain things to him, maybe he'll testify against him. From the sound of things, Larry doesn't want any part of this.*

Bang! Creek! Gary worked. "Hand me the big screw driver."

As Don was backing away from the window, he accidentally scooted a chair a few inches across the linoleum floor. *Damn!* He froze where he was. Then holding his breath, he tiptoed quickly into the next room and let the air out.

"Hey! Shh! Listen," Larry said, tapping Gary on the shoulder. "What?"

"I thought I heard something."

"Ahh! You're just spooked, that's all. The old broad ain't home. We both watched her leave. We know what kind of car she drives, and we know where she went. It even looked like she had an overnight bag with her, so she probably won't be back, tonight anyway. Shine that light down here, I can't see."

"How much more you got to do to get that wood off of there?" Larry asked nervously. "The sooner the better. I'm gettin' a bad feeling about this whole mess."

"I think I almost got it," Gary told him.

Bang! Bang! Bang! Creek! Creek!

"Here it comes," Gary said and tossed some of the wood out of the way. "Ouch!" Larry yelled as a nail in one of the pieces gouged his leg.

"Stop your damn whinin' and give me the small hand shovel. You know the boys in the big house like it when you whine and whimper like that," Gary chided and crawled under the porch. About one minute later, he tossed the large soil-covered trash bag out of the hole, and then crawled out behind it. "This is it, little brother. This one didn't even get wet. Here you carry it." As he picked up the tools . . .

"Sheriff's office! Stop what you're doing and put your hands in the air," John ordered. "Right now! Hands in the air."

All in one motion, Gary turned and threw the shovel and the hammer in John's face, throwing him off balance.

John managed to duck the shovel, but the hammer hit him right in the nose. Blood went everywhere; his eyes swelled shut immediately. He was down for the count.

John had snuck up on them so quietly that Don didn't even know he was there until he heard him telling them to put their hands in the air. By the time Don pulled his gun out of the holster and opened the back door, Gary was already running up the path at the north corner of the yard with the trash bag slung over his shoulder. Don fired two shots but missed him. Gary had disappeared into the woods. When he turned around, Larry was standing there with his hands in the air.

"John's hurt pretty bad," he told Don.

"Put your hands down, son, and help me. Go in the house and call the operator, tell her where we are and to send the paramedics."

"Yes, sir!" he said and ran into the house. He turned on the lights and went to the telephone.

"John? . . . John! Can you hear me?"

"Mmm! Sigh! Starry, boss! He surprised da ell ou'da me. Oh ban. I can see a-ting. Whad he hed me wid?"

"Here, I am going to get you in the house where it's warm. Don't talk, just hold on. Larry, give me a hand here! Please," he shouted.

Larry came down the back steps to help. "They're on the way," he said.

They took him to a chair in the kitchen. "Go in the bedroom and get a couple blankets."

"Yes, sir."

When he came back with the blankets, Don told him to put one on the floor. He needed to lie down. "Here, help me with him." With Larry on one side and Don on the other, they lowered John to the floor.

Larry covered John with the other blanket and went to the refrigerator and got some ice out of the freezer. He fished through the drawers until he found a sandwich bag and put some of the ice cubes in it. "Here put this on the bridge of his nose. It'll help the swelling."

"Looks like you've had experience with this kind of thing."

"Yah! With a brother like mine, you learn to survive. It looks like I'm in a lot of trouble, doesn't it?"

"Well! From what I heard, you're a victim here too."

"Then I did hear something."

"Yah, I blew it. But seriously if you tell the authorities what you know about this, then we can put him away for life without a chance for parole. All the good behavior in the world isn't going to set free somebody that attacked an officer of the law."

"Then I don't have to go to jail for helping him and knowing what he did?" "That's right, son. You have my word, if that means anything to ya."

"Yes! Yes! Yes, it does! It means a lot. I thought he was full of it when he said all those things, but I've learned not to argue with him. He thinks I'm stupid, but I'm not. He's a lot stronger than I am though, and he always gets his way."

"Not after we get through with him. Do we have a deal?"

"We do," Larry said, holding out his hand and shaking Don's. "I can even tell you how he got the money, and how many people he's killed, if what he said is true. Which I think *is* true. He's never lied to me that I know of, that is, except what he said to me a little while ago, about me going to jail. He probably told me that to scare me into doing what he wanted me to."

"I believe you're right about trying to scare you, but I have a feeling that he's scared too. Do you have any idea where he went to? I know that there's a trail or path back there. Where does it lead to?"

"Our old tree house is about three hundred yards into the woods, in a big old walnut tree. He's more than likely gone from there by now. He's driving my Cadillac. No, wait a minute!" Larry said, fishing through his pockets. "I've still got the keys."

"That doesn't mean a thing, son, he'll hot-wire it."

"Then, we can get him for car theft too!" Larry added excitedly. "Now that's the spirit!"

"Oh God! John! What happened to him?" asked Deputy Sara Forester from the back door, with gun in hand.

Behind her was Deputy Bill Thompson. "Dear God!"

"Gary Johnson did this. This is his brother Larry, and he's volunteered to help us find him. I want an APB [All Points

Bulletin] out on him. Here's the make and model of the car," he said, pointing to the paperwork on the table. "The registration says it was sold to Larry Johnson, but Gary stole it from him," Don said, looking at Larry, giving him a nod. You're doing the right thing, son."

"I know I am, sir," Larry confirmed.

"Gentlemen, get your flashlights out. Larry's going to show you where the tree house is. And we need to confirm that the car is gone before we put out the APB on it."

"Tree house? Sir?"

"It's where he's been staying since he got out of jail," Larry told them. "He's probably not there anymore, but I'll show you anyway. Maybe you can find some clues or something."

"Before you leave, what took you guys so long to get here?" Don asked.

"We were called to an accident. Two people were hurt, not wearing their seat belts. We got the call to come out here, just as the ambulance was leaving. The driver at fault wasn't hurt, but we had to take him back to the jail. He was drunk [DUI]."

"OK. Get on out to the tree house and see what you can find."

"Right this way, guys, we need to go through the back yard to get there," Larry said, pointing out the back door.

"After you."

Don was still sitting on the floor next to John when the paramedics arrived.

They knocked on the front door. Don yelled, "Come around the back!"

When the medic took the ice bag off. There was the distinct pattern of a hammer (side view, claw and all) across the bridge of John's nose and up onto his forehead. "Well! We don't have to ask what they hit you with." Then he went on to ask John the usual questions, about how many fingers and so on while he took John's vital signs.

While the young man worked on John, Don asked the other medic how Becka Freeman was. He was one of the paramedics that had picked her up earlier that day. Did they have any word on her condition? "They're both going to be fine. She's going to be sore and bruised. They're keeping her overnight just to be sure, mostly for baby."

"That's great! The same guy that did that to her did this dirty deed too." "What is he, on a rampage? I hope you catch up to him before he leaves us a DOA [Dead on Arrival]."

"Rampage is a good word for it. Can you believe that the guy is out on good behavior?"

"Oh man! Seems like things are getting crazier all the time."

"Looks like I'm going to have to ask for reinforcements till we get this guy. He's stone-cold crazy, out of his mind. His own brother is anxious to see him locked up."

"Yah! Things are in a pretty sad state of affairs. Well, let's get him on the stretcher and get him out of here. This gentleman is going to be in the hospital for a while. Looks like he's got a concussion. He's seeing double."

When they had gone, Don had the sad duty of calling John's wife and telling her that her husband had been taken to the hospital. "Hello, Laura. This is Don . . . Just fine, dear . . . Listen to me. John's on his way to the hospital . . . Yes, he's going to be fine . . . About a half hour ago . . . He got hit in the head and it broke his nose . . . With a hammer . . . No, he got away . . . Yes. Everybody is out looking for him now . . . I know, dear. Try to calm down now. Take a deep breath. He's going to be OK . . . He's got a hard head, remember? . . . Maybe your mother can come over to watch the kids. She lives close by, doesn't she? . . . That's good . . . Are they awake? . . . Let 'em sleep, you can tell them in the morning . . . I'm sure she will . .

. Maybe your dad should drive you down there . . . I'll see you there . . . I'm coming down there after I'm finished here . . . Good bye, dear."

Now he had to call Joanne.

. . .

Lilly and Joanne were watching a television show on the Animal Channel. It was called *Pet Rescue*. There was a dog stuck in a narrow space, between a brick wall and the wall of a house. "Oh look, he's so frightened. The poor thing."

Ring! Ring!

"Tong!"

"That's probably Don," Lilly said as she answered the telephone.

"I hope everything is OK over there," Joanne added.

"Me too. Hello!" Lilly listened carefully and then said, "OK. I'll let her know . . . Yes, I will . . . I'm sorry to hear that . . . Tell him I'll come by to see him tomorrow . . . Thanks for calling . . . Sure, good bye."

"Was that Don?"

"Yes, it was, and the guy got away."

"Oh great! Now what are we going to do?"

"He said that they apparently got what they came for. He doesn't see any reason for them to come back, but not to come home tonight. It's a crime scene now and they need to photograph everything."

"Well! I didn't plan on going back there tonight anyway."

"Ting."

"He said to keep everything locked up here tonight."

"Ting!"

"The guy is a real nut case. I know him. His name is Gary Johnson. He almost killed his wife. Ex-wife now. That's why he was in jail, but he's out on good behavior. Go figure that one."

"Such violence! I just don't understand. I thought I'd get away from it up here, away from the big city."

"He went over to her house earlier today and beat her up. If it hadn't been that her new husband came home when he did, I think he would have finished the job," she said and then added. "John, that's one of the deputies, got hurt tonight when he tried to stop him. The guy hit him in the head with a hammer. I'm going to visit him tomorrow, and then check with his wife to see if she needs anything. They have two kids."

"Then he is dangerous. Is the deputy going to be all right?" "As far as Don could tell, yes."

"I wonder what was so important that they came back again," Joanne said. "I certainly hope they got everything so they *don't* come back. Didn't you say 'he' got away? What about the other one? You did say 'they,' didn't you?"

"Yes. His brother's name is Larry. He's a nice enough guy, but his brother always bullied him into doing whatever he wanted him to do. If he didn't, then Gary would keep hitting him until he gave in. Don just told me that Larry is helping them catch his brother. I guess, while Gary was in jail, he had time to find out what it's like to live a normal life. He's jumping at the chance to get him out of his life for good," Lilly told her.

"What if he gets out on good behavior again? I know the jails are doing that because of the overcrowding."

"Not this time. Attacking an officer of the law, and Don said that he killed some people. He was bragging about to his brother. Held up an armored bank truck."

"Oh WOW!"

"Tong!"

"Excuse me again. I'm going to check all the windows."

CHAPTER 7

Gary stopped and looked back for his brother. *There he is, just standin' there with his hands in the air. I told him to run, that stupid little shit. Well that'll teach him. I told him he's not going to like it in jail.*

One of the shots that the sheriff fired at him clipped his left shoulder. It was bleeding all over his shirt. And it stung like crazy.

After he figured out that they weren't following him, he made his way to the tree house and managed to toss all of his things down to the ground. After putting everything in the trunk, he pulled out a somewhat clean shirt and a towel for a bandage. He changed his shirt and stuffed the towel inside over the wound. When he got in the car, he discovered that there were no keys. *Damn that little turd. I told him to leave the keys in the car. Ain't nobody gonna steal it out here. Wait till I get hold of you.* "You'll be sorry!" he shouted at the top of his lungs. His shoulder was hurting even more now. He had a hard time hot-wiring the ignition, but after a few tries, he got the car started.

. . .

"Did you hear something?" Deputy Sara Forester said as they struck out on the trail.

"Sounds like my brother. I don't know what he said, but I can tell by his voice that he's pissed off. I've got the car keys."

"He's probably got it hot-wired by now," said Deputy Bill Thompson. "He'll be gone before we get there," Larry told them.

They all picked the pace up a bit and started running. This proved to be difficult in the dark, even with flashlights to show the way. Small branches and leaves seemed to reach out for them, slapping their faces as they passed by. About twenty feet from the tree house, Larry pointed and said, "There it is, just up ahead."

"Where? I don't see it," Sara said

"Shine your light up into that walnut tree," Larry instructed as he continued to point.

"Oh! Neat!" Bill said. "That is cool. I've never been in a tree house before.

Who built it for you?"

"I did most of the work. Gary did most of the bossing."

"Looks like you did a good job. A roof, a door, and windows," Bill commented. "How long did it take to build it?"

"We started with a platform and kept adding on to it for about a year or so. Gary did help with the heavy pieces. I'm only five foot ten and a half, and he's like six three and outweighs me by a hundred pounds."

"Five ten isn't short, but six three is extra tall. Just remember that *size* doesn't make the man," Bill said as they approached with their guns drawn.

"The car's not here," Larry said and walked over to the tire tracks. "Shine the light over here. Thanks. There's blood on this shirt he left behind. Looks like he's been shot in the shoulder." Picking it up, he said, "Left shoulder. I hope it slows him down some. He can really move when he wants to. Mom always said that, 'He can disappear quicker than lightning when there's chores to do.'"

"Well let's get a look inside. See if he left anything behind," Bill said excitedly. He was anxious to climb inside.

"Go ahead. I'm going to check out this stuff on the ground," Sara said, shining her flashlight around on the grass and ferns that surrounded the area.

What they found was mostly trash, but there were some interesting-looking bits and pieces of paper too. "What in the world? Is this what I think it is? It looks like somebody tore up some money. It's dirty too."

"That's part of the money that was in the first bag we dug up. It had several holes in it, and the money got wet and moldy. When we tried to pull it apart, it was kind of mushy like old wet newspaper it just *fell* apart. Gary was really pissed off about it too. This time he couldn't blame me. It had bugs and worms in it too," Larry told them.

"Hey! Check this out," Bill said as he tossed down a stack of money that was still in the bank binder strap. "There's a bunch of it up here."

Larry caught it. "See! This is what I was saying. Look at this." He squeezed the stack, and dirty water dripped to the ground. When he opened his hand, the bills were a wad in pulp and mold. It was hardly recognizable as money.

"WOW! I've never seen that happen to money before. Just drop it on the ground. We'll get a lab team out here to pick everything up. They have a way of figuring out how much is there and where it came from."

"That's good, 'cause I wouldn't have any idea how to begin to do that." "Me neither. Those lab guys have equipment that can tell them just about anything, about anybody," Sara said and then shouted, "Hey, Bill! Anything else up there?"

"Nah! Just some empty food containers, that's all . . . Wait, there's something under the mattress. Hold on . . . There's a purse. I'm going to open it," he shouted down to Larry and his partner.

Larry and Sara stood there looking up at the tree house. "A purse? I wonder if he had a girl up there? That would be against *his* rules. He always said that we were never to bring strangers here. Heck! Our folks never knew about this place," Larry said.

Bill climbed about halfway down the ladder and dropped to the ground. "Look at this," he said, holding an empty open wallet in one hand, and the purse in the other.

"Anything in the purse?" Sara asked.

"Here!" Bill said, handing the purse to Sara. "You check it. I just took the wallet out."

"Let's put the wallet back inside and show this to the sheriff," Sara said, holding out the open purse for the wallet. "Let's get back and tell him what we found," she said, picking up a couple pieces of torn money.

On the way back to the old Johnson place, they searched the ground just as a matter of routine, but found nothing out of the ordinary, except some blood here and there on the path. "He doesn't appear to be bleeding too much," Larry said. "Maybe the bullet just grazed him. Most of the blood was on that shirt he left back there."

They continued walking and looking without speaking until Bill asked Larry, "I've seen you at the hardware store, haven't I? Do you work there?"

"Yes!" he said proudly. "Been there almost three years. Gonna get a bonus this year. I think I did a job for your dad last month. Matthew Thompson? His garage door opener had to be replaced."

"Oh yah! He told me about it. He said that I should ask you to help me build some patio furniture next spring. He said you do pretty good work."

"He asked me if I was interested. Told him to have you call me when you're ready."

"I'll do that, for sure. Seems like there's not enough time to get everything done that needs to be. This job and I'm taking some 'home study' classes. They take a lot of my time."

Sara interrupted, "I need to add another bedroom onto my house. The kids are growing so fast. We've already got the foundation done, but it's like Bill said, 'It's hard to find the time.'"

"I'd be more than happy to come over. See how far you've gone and what's left to do. Let's just get my brother put away first. He has a way of fouling up every single thing I do."

"That's a deal," Sara said as they entered Joanne's backyard and headed for the door.

"Come on in, boys. What have you got there?" Don said, looking at the articles that Sara was carrying.

"These were inside the tree house. The purse was under a mattress and there's a lot more of this money around, inside and outside on the ground."

"It's the money from the first bag I was telling you about, Sheriff," Larry added.

Bill told Don, "There wasn't any ID in the wallet I took out of the purse, it was empty. Put it back inside."

Don picked up the purse and emptied the contents on the kitchen table.

"Hey! This is Becka's key chain," Larry almost shouted.

"How do you know what her key chain looks like?" Don demanded.

Larry held it out for them to inspect. "Tom had me engrave her name on the back of this metal heart. I've got one of those electric pencils down at work," he said, turning it over for them. "See?" Then the expression on his face turned to shear panic. "Oh my god!" he yelled. "There's no keys on here. Gary's got Becka's house keys. He'll hurt her if he gets the chance. He just as well had, told me he would. He's pissed off about the divorce. Somebody's got to call over there and warn them. Tell Tom . . ."

"He's already been there," Don said.

"Oh God, nooo!" Tears immediately came to his eyes. "Is she . . . is she . . ." The words wouldn't come out of his mouth.

"She's going to be all right. Bruised and sore."

"The baby! Is the baby OK?" Larry was close to frantic by now. Tears dripping onto his shirt. He loved Becka and her new family. "I'll kill him, that no-good . . ."

"Take a number," Don said, trying to keep this man from going over the edge. To him, Larry looked like he had reached the breaking point. It was obvious that Gary had put him through hell these last few days. Not to mention having to grow up with Gary as the big bully brother. Now Gary was hurting the ones that Larry loved. Larry just drew a mental line in the sand, dirt, pavement, or . . . One more stunt from Gary and there was no telling what Larry would try to do. Enough was enough. "Easy son. Easy! Let's do this the right way. Let me and my boys handle it. Don't go gettin' yourself into trouble, he's not worth it. Don't let him take away everything that you've worked so hard to build. Don't give him another feather in his cap." The best way to fight him is in the witness chair when we get him into court."

Yes! . . . Of course . . . You're right," Larry said, loosening the grip he had on the edge of the table. "He's not gettin' one more thing from me, not my life or my loved ones." He stood with resolution and straightened his shoulders. "What do we do next, Sheriff? Anything. You name it." He spoke like a determined man.

"Slow down there. We're going to take this one step at a time. We need to do this right. We don't want to leave *any* loopholes for him to slip through. With the way that some lawyers work the courts nowadays, he could walk. We're going to gather every scrap of evidence we can get our hands on. Now we're all tired. Let's get some rest and start clear headed in the morning. Me?

I'm going to go home and take a shower and fall in bed. He won't be hanging around here tonight. I'll lock up here tonight and see everybody in the morning."

CHAPTER 8

He made it to the main road and was heading away from town. There weren't any lights on in Becka's house. He pulled into the driveway, turned the lights out, and drove into the backyard. *Where is the bitch?* He knocked on the back door and looked in a couple of the windows. Nobody was home. He was in a rage. Using Becka's keys, he opened the back door. After he got inside, he opened the refrigerator pulling items out and dropping them on the floor. Leftovers, food, milk, and juice all over the floor. He ate lunch meat and cheese right out of the package, grabbed a bottle of wine, and took it in to the bedroom. He stood by the bed, buried his face in each pillow one after the other until he found the one with her perfume on it. The jasmine filled his head with memories. He opened the wine and drank half the bottle at once. Then he proceeded to pour the rest of it all over the bed. He just stood there watching the wine soak into the blankets and laughing. "See how you like this, bitch," he said and threw the empty bottle at the large mirror above the dresser, shattering it into pieces. He proceeded to empty all of their drawers and closets, ripping and tearing as he went. After the bedroom, he went through the house breaking picture frames, tearing pictures, smashing lamps and knick-knacks, slashing furniture, destroying everything in sight. Then he went into the bathroom and released his bowels in the bathtub and urinated on the walls, toilet paper, and towels. He found a first-aid kit and stuffed it in his jacket, keeping that for himself. Then he left the house and drove away, happier than he'd been in a long time.

. . .

After driving a short time, the car sputtered to a stop. Out of gas. He got out and shoved it into a clump of bushes on a small road, downhill from the main highway. He got back in the car and used the first-aid kit to fix his shoulder. It was starting to hurt real bad now, but the bleeding had stopped. "There, that's better. My little exercise workout fixed things up real good. Of course the wine helps too." He closed his eyes and tried to rest, but his mind was still in second gear, working itself up to third. His rage had not yet been satisfied. "Where in the hell is Becka? Probably out with that SOB havin' dinner or something. Well! They've got a big surprise waiting for them. Hope they like it. He he! Ha ha ha!" He laughed for almost a full thirty seconds. "Well they deserved it. Enjoy!"

He got out of the car, grabbed the flashlight, slipped into his backpack, being careful not to let the strap ride on his injured shoulder. Then he slung the strap of his sleeping bag over his right shoulder and started walking into the woods. He had spent many childhood hours hiking and camping in these woods and he knew his way around. After walking for about fifteen minutes, he stopped to rest. *Damn shoulder! You're going to get yours too, Don. Don't you worry! You'll get yours like everybody else around here.*

. . .

He had fallen asleep. When he opened his eyes, he immediately closed them against the pain in his shoulder. The cold from the ground had seeped into it, making it stiff and painful. "Damn it! Mmm! Ahh!" He forced it into movement by drawing an increasingly large circle with his left elbow. Then he checked it for bleeding. It seemed OK, but the pain wasn't going away. Infection crossed his mind, but he pushed it away. "Nah! It'll be OK in a couple days. It's just sore, that's all," he convinced himself.

"Lilly Patterson. Now there's a sweet little package. I'll bet she could keep me warm. Yah! 'Lilly the Filly.'" He reflected on seeing her around town every summer when she visited her grandparents. "Her grandfather isn't around anymore to keep the men away. I'll bet she'd like some company." He was talking to himself now, doing a good job of fooling himself into thinking grand thoughts about himself. "I've always wanted some of that." As he walked along under a black sky filled with oceans of stars and a pail sliver of a moon, he was unaware of the beauty above him. His mind was already full of his next conquest. He was always full of himself, but now it was intertwined with insanity. "Eat your heart out, Becka!"

. . .

Lilly and Joanne had stayed up talking until about two in the morning. "Look at the time!" Joanne said. "I really am enjoying myself, but tomorrow or today rather is going to be a very busy day. I need my beauty sleep. I might have to reschedule my dentist appointment again, like I had to this morning, er, I mean yesterday." She yawned.

"Mmm! You're right," Lilly said and stretched while looking at the wall clock. "Let's get some shut-eye. You can use the bathroom first if you like. I'm going to make sure that everything is turned off and tend to the fireplace before I turn in."

"OK! Good night, dear!" They hugged each other like mother and daughter. Something they both needed. "Don't stay up too late, now."

"Yes, Mother!" Lilly teased. "Good night!" They both smiled at each other.

Heading for the bedroom first, Lilly took the crystal out of the pouch and laid it on the nightstand next to the clock radio. Then she slipped out of her jeans and shirt and put on her bathrobe and she went about turning lights off and rechecking the windows.

"Good night, Grandpa."

"Ting!" Sparkle. Twinkle.

She went into the bathroom to wash her face and brushed her teeth. "Tong!"

She didn't hear it. The water was running in the sink. "Tong!"

. . .

Familiarity was his guide tonight. Gary was making good time walking through the woods. He hasn't been in these woods for at least three maybe four years. "There it is," he told himself. He walked around the property just inside the tree line to make sure she was alone. When he was able to see the front yard, he saw no vehicles. *Probably in the garage.*

What he didn't know was that Lilly had Joanne put her car in the garage after they heard that Gary was on the loose. He had obviously been watching her house, so he would know what kind of car she drove. "Let's not take any chances."

"All alone. Huh, baby? Well, fear not. You're about to have company." He walked around the outside of the cabin looking in windows, checking to see if he could gain entry. *Damn! No surprise tonight.*

The light had just gone out in what he figured was the bedroom. The cabin was dark now. He slipped the blade of his Buck knife behind the telephone line and pulled gently upward, severing the line.

. . .

When she opened the bathroom door, she heard it.
"Tong!"
"What's wrong? Is Joanne all right?
"Ting!"
"Are we in danger?"
"Ting!"
Her heart immediately sped up its pace. "Is somebody here?"
"Ting!"
"Inside?"
"Tong!"
"Outside then."
"Ting!"
Lilly immediately turned the bedroom light off and went to the telephone in the living room to call the sheriff's office. She started dialing, then realized that the phone was dead.

Just as she was putting the receiver down, she saw a shadow move across the window next to the front door. Then the door handle clicked. Somebody was trying to get in. It was the kind that you grab hold of the vertical handle and press your thumb down on the lever to release the latch. When it was locked, the only thing you could do was press down, but nothing else would move. It was a good heavy-duty lock. Nobody could come through the door if you didn't want them to. There were three doors in the cabin. Front and back were alike, the one in the workshop was bigger, newer, and not part of the original design of the cabin. She didn't think that it was necessary to have a super heavy-duty door put in her workshop. All she had wanted was a large door so she could move her projects in and out of the workshop without carrying them through the living quarters. There weren't any more bears or mountain lions around like when this cabin was first built ninety-two years ago by her great-grandfather. Now she truly wished that she hadn't had the door added to the cabin at all. It was one of those hollow, insulated kind that kept out the cold, but that's about all. It had a good lock on it, but the door could be broken into if you were strong enough. She had told herself that if she ever lost her keys, she could break in through that door. She ran into the workshop and wedged a chair under the outside door handle. Then she did the same thing to the door to the workshop inside the cabin.

Joanne! Oh my god, I forgot about her. I'd better wake her up before anything else happens. She tapped lightly on the bedroom door and whispered, "Joanne." She tiptoed to the bed and put her hand over her friend's mouth to keep her from crying out if she were to be startled. Joanne's eyes opened immediately. "Joanne. It's Lilly. We have to be quiet. Somebody is outside of the cabin trying to get in. I'm going to get dressed. Quickly now! You do the same thing. Dress warm, we may have to leave the cabin." Then she left the room.

"Tong! . . . Tong! . . . Tong!"

"Yes I know! Thank you," she said as she took the .357 Smith and Wesson out of the drawer next to her bed, then went into the living room and got the 9mm Mauser out of the drawer in the table next to the fireplace. She was checking to make sure that they were both loaded when Joanne tiptoed into the room.

"What do we do now?" Joanne said under her breath.

"Which one of these do you want?" she whispered, showing both to her.

"I'm familiar with the revolver. I have one just like it," she whispered, holding out her hand.

"There's not much we can do, but wait to see if he tries anything. The telephone is dead. Whoever it is probably cut the line."

"Do you think that it's that Gary person?"

"Ting!"

"I'll bet it is. We don't usually get this kind of trouble up here." *Crash! Tinkle!*

"Tong! Tong!"

"There goes the window in my workshop. I put a chair against the door. Guess he decided that the window was easier."

"Ahh!" Gary shouted with the pain in his shoulder as he slid through the window. The broken glass sliced his pant leg, cutting his thigh. Now his leg was bleeding, not too bad, but it was stinging like crazy. His shoulder was hurting again too. He stood there silently, holding his breath and biting his lip against the pain. His anger was taking over him again. The pain was secondary. He ran full force and threw his body against the door that led out of the workshop into the cabin. *Thud! . . . Bang!* He hit the door and then fell to the floor. The pain returned to him, doubled. "Argh! Bitch! Open this door. NOW! I won't hurt you if you'll just open the door. I'm hurt and I need your help. Damn it!" The chair on the other side was doing its job.

"Who are you?" Lilly shouted through the door.

"It's me, Lilly. It's Gary Johnson."

"Why didn't you just knock on the door?"

"I did, but you didn't answer."

"Tong!"

"No, you didn't."

"Yes, I did. Honest! I tried the handle after I thought nobody was home." "Why did you break my window?"

"I told you I'm hurt, bitch! Aren't you listening? I thought I could find some first-aid stuff in here, that's all."

"OK. You're hurt. Stay right there. I'm going to the phone and I'm going to call for an ambulance," Lilly said and put her finger to her lips and motioned for Joanne to follow her into the next room. "I'll be right back."

"The telephone is dead," Joanne whispered.

"I know that, and he knows that. He doesn't know that I know that. He also doesn't know that I'm not alone, or that we have two guns."

"I don't know if I could shoot anybody."

"If your life depends on it, you won't have any trouble at all. Remember, this guy has already killed three people. That's what Don said."

"Well I guess so."

"We don't have to kill him. Just stop him. Aim for an arm or a leg. That should slow him down."

"He said he was hurt. What if that's true?" Joanne asked.

"I don't know just yet. I'm going to talk to him again," she said and walked back into the other room with Joanne close behind.

"There's something wrong with my phone, Gary. It's not working. Gary, are you still there?"

"Yes! Where else would I be? I told you I'm hurt. My leg's bleeding pretty bad. I cut it on the window."

"OK! Wait a minute. I'll be right back." She took Joanne into the other room and told her the plan. "Are you sure you can do this? My life depends on it. If you have any doubts, tell me right now and we'll figure something else out."

"I can do it. It seems OK to me, but only if you're sure."

"Yes! I am. Let's get this over with," Joanne said, pulling her shoulders back with courage.

CHAPTER 9

At four thirty in the morning when Thomas got home from the hospital, everything seemed normal until he unlocked the door and tried to push it open. It seemed to be stuck shut. "That's odd. It shouldn't be warped shut. It hasn't rained for about two weeks." He put his shoulder to it and pushed. Nothing. He walked around to the back door wondering what else could go wrong. The doctor was keeping Becka in the hospital for another two days, maybe three. The baby was under stress, and Becka needed to stay off of her feet, with complete bed rest. He and the doctor agreed that it would be better for her to stay. If she came home, she would be trying to do things for herself.

When he stepped into the kitchen, his shoe crunched on broken glass. "What is this?" he said and flipped the light switch by the back door. "Oh my god." He knew immediately what had happened and picked up the wall phone next to the door.

"Sheriff's office. Deputy McClelland."

"This is Thomas Freeman. I need to speak to Sheriff Wilson."

"He's not in the office right now. How can I help you, Mr. Freeman?" "Gary Johnson trashed my house. Don wanted me to let him know the minute I heard anything about him."

"Are you sure that it was him?"

"Yes. It couldn't have been anybody else. He has injured my wife and child, and he threatened my life."

"OK, sir. I've got a unit on the way and I'm calling the sheriff right after we hang up. I'll have him call you right back. Give me your phone number."

Thomas gave his number and hung up the phone. He tiptoed around the mess in the kitchen and stepped over and walked around broken pictures and slashed furniture in the living room. It was then that he discovered why he couldn't get the front door open. The couch had been pushed up against it, and the television was on the couch, with a broken picture tube. Tears came to his eyes when he entered the bedroom. Gary had used one of Becka's lipsticks to write on the wall above the bed, "DIE BITCH," and then under that, "LOVE GARY." Then there was a picture of a hanged man on the gallows just like the one in the word game "Hang Man." This one showed a knife in the chest with dripping blood. Suddenly Thomas went on alert. "Are you still here, you bastard?" He looked around. Nothing. "How come you always do your dirty work when the real man is gone? Huh? Tell me that. You're a coward, that's why." At that moment, he was glad that Becka wasn't here to see this.

Ding! Dong! The doorbell rang.

"Who is it?" he shouted.

"It's Don."

"Come to the back door!" he shouted again, as he made his way back to the kitchen.

"Oh my god, look at this," Don said as he stepped into the house. "Do we know for sure it was Gary?"

"Yeah! He left a note in the bedroom. Come on, I'll show you," he said, leading the way.

"Oh man! This guy is really bent in the head. Where's Becka? How's she doing?"

"She's still at the hospital. The baby's in stress. If anything else happens, I'm . . . I'm going to have a hard time keeping my promise to let you handle it."

"Lilly!"

Don turned to see who had just spoken. "Did you hear that?"

"Hear what? Is somebody here?" Thomas walked into the living room. "Hello." Nothing. Then he went to check the rest of the house.

"Help Lilly!"

Don has had voices talk to him ever since he almost died a few years back. He had been in an accident and was hospitalized for seven weeks with a head injury. He didn't hear them all the time. Only on rare occasions. Over the years, he had learned to listen to the voices. Right now he knew that he had to get to Lilly's cabin. How could he explain this to Thomas? He couldn't.

Thomas came back into the room. "Nothing."

"Probably just hearing things. It is rather spooky walking into this mess."

Within a few minutes, they heard, *Ding! Dong!*

Don grabbed the opportunity to leave Thomas alone. "That's my men. I see their light bar flashing through the window. I'll go talk to them. You stay here. I'll tell them to come around to the back."

Don went out the back door and told the two deputies to take a report of the damage. He was headed for Lilly Patterson's cabin if they needed him for anything else.

"Right, boss!" They headed for the back door as Don got into his patrol car.

He called his office on the radio and had them place a call to Lilly's place. To warn her that Gary was on the rampage. The call didn't go through. Something was wrong with the telephone. The operator tried twice and still nothing. There wasn't any traffic so he didn't put the siren or the light bar on, but he sped in her direction as quickly as he could make the car go.

. . .

Gary was standing facing the door with his gun pointed straight ahead. Lilly had agreed to open the door. This little filly was his tonight. Nobody could stop him now. "What are you waiting for, I promised not to hurt you if you help me. I'm bleedin' pretty bad here. Come on before I pass out. Pleeease!"

Lilly tucked her gun in the back of her pants' waist and pulled her jacket down over it. Then pulled the chair away from the door. "Stand back now. I'm going to open the door."

"OK! Hurry, please!"

After she pulled the door open, she froze, staring at the gun pointed at her chest. "You said that I could trust you. Why the gun, Gary?" she said, holding out her empty hands.

"Just my insurance that you weren't tryin' to trick me."

"Why would I do that? I didn't even know that you were in town. Is your jail sentence over already? Man! Time sure flies, doesn't it?" Then trying to look shocked at the sight of his injuries, she said, "Oh WOW! Come here and let me take care of that for you. Were you in an accident or something? You poor thing. Sit down here at the table. That looks pretty bad." She pulled the chair out that she wanted him to sit in. "And put that gun down, silly. Big man like you afraid of me? You did say that you're not going to hurt me if I help you. Didn't you?"

"Yeah, but how come you're dressed to go outside?"

"Well?" she chastised him, looking at the gun.

He laid it on the table but kept his right hand next to it. "I asked you how come you're dressed like that."

"That's better. Relax! I was just getting ready to leave the house. I was going up north to visit friends. If you had been here twenty minutes later, you would have missed me." She lied. "Now let me look at your leg first. You're gonna have to pull your pants down a bit so I can see it better."

"All right, but no funny stuff." He stood and released his belt and dropped his pants. He was wearing boxer shorts.

The smell coming off of him was making her eyes water. Keeping her back side away from him, she bent over to get a large bowl out of the cupboard and filled it about half full of warm water. Then she pulled the whole roll of paper towels out of the holder and set both items on the table next to the gun as if it belonged there. "Don't shoot me if this hurts, OK?" she said as she dipped about three towels onto the water and proceeded to wash the cut on his leg.

"Ouch! Damn it!" He jerked his leg away. "Take it easy, it feels like you're cuttin' me."

"Ahh! Damn! There must still be some glass in it. Let me look closer." She bent down to get a better look. She could see that he was becoming aroused and his breath was coming out in shaky little bursts. *I'll bet this guy gets off on pain.* "Ahh! There it is," she said, plucking it out with her thumb and fingernails. "See?" She worked quickly, trying not to give him too much pleasure or pain. "It isn't bleeding hardly at all anymore now that the glass is out."

"Thanks. It's feeling better all the time." He smiled and put his hand on her head.

She stood up quickly and his hand slid away. "Now let's look at your arm."

He unbuttoned his jacket, then his shirt, pulling both away, exposing the wound.

She pulled the soiled towel away and inhaled sharply. "Oh my god, Gary! This is infected. How long have you had this?" she said with all the sympathy she could muster.

"Couple days."

Lilly wasn't about to say that it looked like a bullet wound. "How ever did this happen. It looks like a big chunk of your shoulder was yanked out or something. Did you tangle with an animal? Looks like whatever it was took a bite and yanked it right out. You poor thing! I don't know if I can fix this," she said with exaggerated concern.

"Just clean it up and put some of those clean towels on it. Wait," he said, reaching into his jacket pocket. "Here's a first-aid kit, there might be some medicine in it you can use, maybe some bandages and tape. Just do what you can. OK?"

"You're very brave. I don't know how you stand the pain. You should get to a doctor, Gary. That looks bad."

"Never mind. Just do what you can," he said, inching his hand closer to the gun.

"Well! I'll try! You gotta hold real still. I know this is going to hurt, but I'll try real hard not make it any worse than it is. OK?" She smiled reassuringly.

"OK! OK! Let's just get this over with. I ain't no baby!"

She put fresh water in the bowl and tore off more paper towels. As she put the towels in the water, she turned her head and coughed. "Excuse me!" She saw Joanne inching her way up close behind him with the .357 and looked quickly away. *The first cough was "get ready" and the second cough was "go."* "Here we go, now hold still." She was talking more to Joanne than Gary. The poor woman looked scared to death but determined to do the job.

She had better act now. She stepped away from Gary and coughed again.

"All right! Don't move a muscle or this .357 will take your head right off your shoulders," Joanne ordered as she put the gun on the back of Gary's neck.

The sudden knowledge that he might die froze him to the spot. *This is an old woman's voice, she won't shoot. Lilly must have given her gun to the old woman, and now she doesn't have one of her own. These bitches are so stupid,* he told himself. His hand was inches from his own gun. Without going for it, he spun in the chair and knocked Joanne off of her feet. The gun went flying, landed on the floor, and fired, hitting the wall. Joanne screamed, covering her ears against the sound of the shot, inches from her head, praying that she or Lilly hadn't been hit, hoping that he would be stopped by the bullet.

Gary stood and ran after the gun, but his pants were pulled down and he went sprawling, face down, flat on the floor. "Oof!" The air was knocked out of him. The bullet whizzed past his head.

Lilly pulled her gun and grabbed his off the table. "Don't move, Gary! I've got two guns on you. Don't move! I ought to shoot you just for hurting my friend!" she yelled. "Joanne, are you all right?" She said over her shoulder, not wanting to look away from Gary.

"Yes! I believe so," she said, rubbing her head.

"Go in the shop and get one of those little rolls of wire. We'll tie him up."

"Ting!"

"Be right back, dear."

"Gary!" she yelled "I told you not to move." "My shoulder hurts. Damn it!"

"Too bad! Lay still or I'll shoot you in your other shoulder, and it won't be just a nick like the other one."

"You knew?"

"Sure! Don Wilson told me about it yesterday. The whole town knows you're out and being bad again. Everybody is looking for you. You can't go anywhere around here that they won't tell the sheriff. Now shut your mouth or I'll tape it shut. You haven't got a thing to say that's worth hearing."

"OK! I'm ready. Let me do it. Pleeease?" Joanne begged.

"Gary, put your hands behind you, and don't give her any trouble."

Joanne put a set of handcuffs on him and stepped over his legs, grabbed his belt, and cinched it tight around his knees. "There you go, young man. I hope it's uncomfortable. How dare you break into my friend's house and threaten her," she said and kicked him in the thigh that was cut.

"Argh! Stop that, bitch."

"Oh dear, it's bleeding on your carpet, but don't worry. I'll clean it up. It's worth it," Joanne said as she kicked him again.

"You want some of this, dear?"

"No! I believe you did just fine. I'll take that second one for me. Where in the world did you find handcuffs?"

. . .

Don turned his headlights off before he pulled into the driveway and switched off the engine and coasted up to the cabin. The only sound being the quiet crunching of gravel. He got out, quietly closed the door just enough to turn the dome light off inside, and crept up to the house. He planned on walking all the way around the outside of the cabin first, but he discovered the cut telephone line, then within a couple feet found the broken window. There wasn't any glass outside, and that told him that it was broken inward from out here.

"Bang!"

"Aw! Damn!" He leaned inside the window and quietly lifted the chair away from the door and unlocked it. Before he could get his head out of the window, Joanne walked in.

She sucked in her breath. "Damn! You scared me to death. We've got everything under control. But I'm really glad to see you," she said, opening the door for him. "Come on in, please. You can put your gun away. Lilly has two pointed at him and I get to tie him up. Wanna watch?" she asked as she plucked a roll of wire off the shelf and turned to leave.

"Wait a second. These will be easier for me to get off of him when I throw him in the jail cell," Don said, handing her his handcuffs.

"Before I take them. How do they work?"

"Oh! Here," he said and then showed her.

"Thanks."

"Now!" he said encouragingly. "Go finish what you started. I'll be right there."

. . .

"Oh yes, I forgot to tell you that Don's here." She smiled in his direction.

Lilly turned to see Don standing in the doorway. "Hi! I think we have somebody here that you have been looking for."

"You might want to give him one more just for me, Joanne." Don laughed. "This is for treating everybody so mean." Joanne lifted her leg back. "And digging that big hole in my backyard." She swung even harder than before. "Bitch!" Gary yelled.

"Excuse me," Joanne said and left the room and returned with a three-inch roll of duct tape. She ripped off a piece and slapped it across his mouth. "The lady told you to shut your mouth or get it taped shut. I'm fulfilling her wishes."

"Good job, Joanne. Thanks!"

"Anytime, dear. Oh my! Look at this. It's not sticking very well to your sweaty skin. Here let me have that," she said and ripped it off of his face.

"Ahhh! You're all going to pay for this. Prisoners have rights."

"Oh dear! Did that hurt? . . . That's good," she said as she wiped his face with his own shirttail. "Here, have another. This one will stay on better," she told him as she applied another piece of tape, then stood and dusted her hands proudly.

"That ought to hold him."

"WOW! I don't think I'll have to be reminded to *never* to get you pissed off at me," Don said.

They all laughed except Gary, who was trying to find a more comfortable position. Don told them about Tom and Becka's house, and what Gary had done to Becka earlier that day.

"Oh my god, Gary! You really are a bastard, aren't you? I hope they hang you from the highest place they can find," Lilly said.

"Ting!"

"Hanging's too good for a monster like him," Joanne added.

"Bastard's the wrong word for him. We really can't blame his parents for that. His folks are nice people. His brother, Larry, won't have to worry about him ruining his life anymore either. He's going to testify in court, when the time comes," Don said.

"That's good." Lilly said. "Larry has always been nice to me. Whenever I go into the hardware store for stuff to build my trinkets with, he helps me find whatever I need. If they don't have it, he brings out the catalogs and orders whatever I need. It's too bad that his brother treated him like he did. Always getting him in trouble."

"He made Larry dig up your backyard to get part of the robbery money that he buried there. Then tonight he got the rest of it from under your back porch. There's some damage but not much. I can help you fix whatever needs to be done," Don said to Joanne. "I also heard him talking to his brother. Gary killed at least three men just to keep all the money for himself. The joke's on him though. The money that was buried got all moldy, so he couldn't spend any of it."

"I'll bet he thought he was really clever when he did that," Lilly commented. "He always acted like he was better than anybody else," Lilly said.

"Do Tom and Becka need a place to stay?" asked Joanne.

"Just until they can fix things up again. Tell him I'm offering."

"I'll do anything that I can to help too," Lilly offered.

"I will, but I believe Tom will be staying at her parents' house. It's not far from here. But I'll tell him that you offered help, both of you," Don assured them.

. . .

After Don locked Gary's cell door, he went into the office and called the paramedics to arrange for a medical examination of the prisoner. Then he called the state prison authorities to come and get Gary Manfred Johnson for parole violations. He was told to contact Gary Johnson's parole officer, and that he (the parole officer) would be making the arrangements for Gary Johnson's transfer and would be contacting the sheriff's office later that morning. Don left the office number, thanked them, and hung up the telephone.

His next job was to go through Gary's personal belongings and itemize what was there. From his pockets, there was some loose change, a Buck knife with a five-inch blade, twelve twenty-dollar bills with a rubber band wrapped around them, four loose keys (probably Becka's)—he set those aside he wanted her to identify them as hers—half pack of cigarettes, a Zippo lighter, and a wallet with his parole officer's card, parole papers, a picture of Becka and himself at their wedding, and a list of phone numbers (this, Don took to the copy machine before returning them to the wallet). After placing these items in a large envelope, Don went through Gary's backpack. There was clothing, underwear, toothbrush, and paste, and several packets of old moldy money. When Don unrolled the sleeping bag, he found three skin magazines. These he added to the list. When he finished this task, he went home and kicked off his shoes and fell in bed without undressing. He was exhausted. It was five o'clock in the morning.

CHAPTER 10

The lab guys arrived at Tom and Becka's house the next day at about ten in the morning. "Oh man! I hope I brought enough film to get all of this." One of the technicians said, "The report said it was a small job."

"It was early this morning when he came back. Typical coward. Do your dirty deeds and run before you get caught. My guess is that he wasn't too upset, 'cause we weren't here," Tom told them. "I haven't touched anything. I'm going to the hospital to see my wife. Don't worry about locking up when you leave."

"Sure! OK! Don't worry, we'll probably still be here when you get back.

There's a lot to do."

"OK then! I'll see you later," Tom said as he left the cottage.

. . .

Earlier that morning, Tom had called his homeowner's insurance company. He had just made the second payment on the premium and was worried that there would be a problem making a claim for so much at one time. After he told them that they had lost all of their personal belongings, they said that the only thing he needed was a copy of the police report and photographs if possible. Don said that he told the lab guys to make sure that he received copies of the photographs and the paperwork. They were to stop by the sheriff's station and make photocopies of everything for Don anyway, so they might as well get an extra copy while they were at it. That should satisfy the insurance company. At least it should speed things up for the settlement.

As he drove, he pondered, *How am I going to tell Becka? I don't want her any more upset than she is already. I need to talk to her parents and the doctor. Maybe together we can figure this thing out. I don't want to lose the baby.* "Dear Lord!" he prayed aloud. "I've always been thankful to you for giving Becka to me to love and care for. Please help me do this right. I'm not sure how to handle this. Don't let anything happen to our baby. Thank you for giving us everything that we have so far, including each other, and our baby. Please help me. I need your guidance. I am leaving whatever happens from this point forward in your hands, Lord. Please guide me. Thank you. Amen." He had to pull over to the side of the road before he finished his prayer because his tears were making it difficult to see. When he regained his composure, he was looking at an abandoned car in the bushes just off the road. *Humm! I'll have to mention this to Don when I see him.* He checked himself out in the mirror and ran his fingers through his long straight black hair. "Thank you, Lord! I feel better already." He started the car and continued his drive to the hospital.

. . .

When Tom arrived at the hospital, he was surprised to see so many people he knew in the waiting room. There was Lilly Patterson, Larry Johnson, Jerry Flowers, Deputies Sara Forester and Bill Thompson, and a lady that he didn't know who was sitting next to Lilly, smiling at him. "Did somebody call a town meeting that I didn't know about?" he asked.

"Just about," Howard Bluefeather said as he walked in behind Tom. "You haven't been living up here very long, but as you can see, we stick together when someone is in need. When we heard about what had happened, there wasn't much that could have kept us away. We're going to do whatever we can to help. Have you met our new neighbor? She moved into the old Johnson place."

"No, I haven't," he said, smiling back at Joanne's contagious smile.

"Step over here a minute," Howard said.

Joanne stood up when they approached her. "Hi, Tom! I'm Joanne Mason," she said as they shook hands. "These nice people have told me about your plight. I'm here to help in any way I can.

"Tom Freeman. It's a pleasure to meet you, and thank you," he said to Joanne. Then he looked around the room, and tears came to his eyes once again. "The Lord has truly blessed me. To have so many friends . . . I just don't know what to say."

Lilly and Sara came to his side, and both of them put an arm around his shoulders. Lilly said, "Hey! This is what friends are supposed to do for each other. Our first job is to make sure that you both know you're not in this alone. That's the hardest part, the rest will be easy with our help." "I just don't know how to tha—"

"Ah ah! That's enough for now. I think Becka needs to see you more than we do. Now go on with you," Sara chided and turned him in the direction of Becka's room.

"Before you go," Bill interrupted. "Some of us that have already seen Becka are going to leave. We'd like to arrange a time to meet over at your place so that we can figure out what needs to be done."

"You guys are right on top of things, aren't you," Tom said.

"We figure to get the worst part of it cleaned up before Becka goes home. She's been told about it, but seeing it is a different story. We know that she needs to stay off of her feet for a while, and if she's anything like me, she won't be able to leave things alone until everything is back to normal," Lilly said.

"God bless you all. Thank you so very much. I'm going to be here for about an hour, but if anybody wants to go over there now, you may see Sheriff Don's lab techs taking pictures of the damages Gary caused. Take my key in case they've left." Said Tom as he removed his house key from his key fob.

"Good idea," Bill said, sticking his hand out for the keys. "We'll see you when you get there. Take your time here. We'll get organized."

"Larry, you need a ride?" Lilly asked. "We can put your bike in the back of my truck."

"Thanks! I near froze my buns off on the way over here. I'll meet you outside."

"Anybody that's not sure where it is, follow me," Sara said. And they all left, except Jerry and Howard who remained seated. They hadn't spoken to Becka yet.

. . .

Becka's doctor met Tom in the hallway outside of Becka's room. "How are they doing, Doctor?"

"She's doing fine, but I believe that it would be best for the baby if she stays here a couple more days. Say! I'm really sorry to hear what happened to your home."

"I was upset about it too on the way over here, but after talking to everybody, it seems that everything is going to be OK," Tom said, blinking back tears that threatened to spill again. "Everybody is being so nice."

"Yes, we have a nice community of folks here. Nobody goes without," the doctor said.

"I'm so glad that the baby is going to be OK. This is really wonderful. I'm going in to see Becka now," Tom said, anxious to leave.

"I'll be talking with you later, Tom."

"Thank you for taking care of her."

"No problem. She's a delightful person to care for."

Don was standing by the bed when Tom walked in.

"Hi, sweetheart! I see you're in good company. How are you feeling?" he asked, nodded to Don, and then bent down to kiss her cheek. "There are quite a few people in the waiting room."

"I'm feeling better than when I got here," she assured him. "Yes, I know about our neighbors being here. The doctor is letting two people at a time come in to talk to me."

"That's nice, honey, but don't get yourself too tired with all this visiting." "I won't, dear. I met our new neighbor Joanne Mason. She seems real nice. She's going to help Larry and the others fix the house up."

"Then you know what he did to it?"

"Yes! Don told me. It's not his fault. I made him tell me, after Lilly mentioned it." She took Tom's hand. "And don't be mad at Lilly either. It's not upsetting me as much as you think.

In fact I expected something like this out of him. He's a violent man. He has been breaking and smashing things as long as I have known him. He was always on his good behavior when he was dating me. I was young and dumb enough to think that I could change his attitude towards other people. That was my mistake when I married him. Our friends are going to help us get things back in order. Aren't they nice?"

"That's good. I'm happy to know that you're not letting his actions upset you. I was really afraid for you to hear the news. Everything is messed up real bad. I thank God that we weren't there when he came back to do his dirty work."

"I'm more angry than upset right now, but don't worry. I'm not going to let anything that Gary's done harm our baby. From what everyone has been saying, I'll be able to follow doctor's orders just fine. It makes me feel better knowing that we have friends and neighbors like them. Did you see all the flowers?"

"They're beautiful, honey. And yes, it makes me feel better, just knowing that there are still nice people in this world. I was feeling pretty depressed on the way over here. I told the Lord while I was driving that I didn't know how to handle things and needed help. When I walked in and saw everybody, my spirits were lifted right away. I knew that he was already helping us before I asked."

"That's good, dear. I've been doing some praying myself. It really helps. In fact Don and I just finished a prayer together before you came in. I just know that everything is going to be better. I feel it in my heart."

"That's great, Don. Thank you for caring."

"Anytime, son. Anytime. We all need a booster shot once in a while."

"We sure do. Oh, that reminds me. On the way over here, I saw an abandoned car in the bushes just off the road, by the turn off to Pioneer Trail Camping Site."

"Yeah? What did it look like?"

"Well. let's see. Only the back end was sticking out. Black or dark blue, older model, maybe 1960-something. Maybe seventies."

"That sounds like the one that Gary was driving. He stole it from his brother. He left Larry behind when he ran. Larry turned the table on him though. He's going to testify against him when we get him into court," Don told them. He pulled out his cell phone, called the office, and told one of his men to get a tow truck out there. "Meet them out there, and make sure that they don't disturb anything, you know the routine." Then he headed for the door and said his good-byes. "I think I'll go out there myself, to make sure they get everything. I'll talk to you later."

"Bye, Don. Thanks again," Tom said.

"Bye!" Becka said and waved.

"Bye, you two," he said and left.

They both agreed that *he's such a nice man*, then just held hands and visited.

"Knock! Knock! Can we interrupt?" It was Jerry and Howard. "We just wanted to pay our respects so we can get on over to your place."

"I'm so sorry! I didn't realize that there was anybody else still waiting. Please! Come on in," Tom said and started to stand up.

"Please stay where you are. We'll only be but a minute. There's a lot of work to do. We're going over to Lilly's to fix a broken window first," Howard said.

"Look, honey! More flowers. You guys are so kind. These are lovely. Thank you so much," Becka said and held them to her nose, inhaling their sweetness.

"You're welcome. Anything for a friend. How are you feeling, Becka?"

"I'm much better thank you. If my Tommy here hadn't come home when he did, I'm sure he would have killed me. Gary's an evil man."

"It's good to see you're feeling better. How long are you going to be in here?" Howard asked.

"The doctor wants to keep me a couple more days, just to make sure the baby is OK."

"That's good, you should be taking it easy anyway," Jerry commented. "Did Gary break the window too?" Becka asked.

"Yeah! Lilly and Joanne had him tied up by the time Don got there," Jerry told them.

"Well! Good! I'm glad that it was women that took him down. Serves him right," Becka said.

"Lilly's a tough cookie. She takes care of herself pretty good," Jerry said proudly.

"Well we're going to go now. We'll see you at the house, Tom," Howard said.

"OK! I'll see you there. Bye!" Tom said.

"Thanks again," Becka said and waved.

. . .

Don arrived just as the tow truck was backing up to the abandoned car.

"That's the car all right. I want to go through it after you pull it out of there," he said to his deputy.

"Sure enough, boss. I'll tell the driver."

While he was waiting, Don followed the tire tracks back up toward the road. *Yep! These are Gary's boot prints. Just like the one at Tom's house and Joanne's.*

"Hey, boss, over here!" the deputy shouted and motioned with his hand. "Look at this before he moves the car."

Under the car was a trash bag. "Pull it out before he moves the car. Let's see what we have here."

As Deputy Gordon tugged on the bag, it ripped open, and out fell more money than either one of them had ever seen. "Wow! Looks like he's been busy since he got out of jail."

"This is the bag he pulled out from under the back porch, over at the house where his parents used to live. "According to his brother, Larry, Gary helped rob an armored truck. There were three of them. They each killed one of the guards and somewhere down the line, Gary killed his partners and took all the money for himself. He buried it in his parents' garden in the backyard and under the porch. He was in the process of retrieving it when John walked up on him."

"Is that when John got hurt?"

"Yeah! He had the hammer in his hand and cold-cocked him with it. By the time I got outside, I only had time to wing him with a shot."

"Oh wow! What happened then?"

"Well! Not much. I was more concerned about John. Larry helped me get him in the house, and then told me what I just told you. I overheard Gary telling him about killing the people involved in the robbery and taking all the money for himself. He claims to have done it for both of them. Told Larry that he didn't have to work anymore. But we know better than that. He just wanted Larry around to do his bidding. He always bullied Larry into doing whatever he didn't want to do himself. Punched him, if he resisted."

"Man! Oh man! We gotta make sure that he *never* gets out again."

"Not to worry! He's not going anywhere after he sees the judge. He had the nerve to tell the kid that he was just as guilty as he was because he knew about it. *And* that he would end up being somebody's sweetheart in jail if they got caught. Tried to intimidate him, so he wouldn't talk," Don told the young deputy.

The young deputy Carl Gordon had been hinting, "Do you need any extra help up here?" And, "I wouldn't mind working up here in God's country." He was one of the extra assistants sent over from the city before Gary was captured. Deputy Gordon wanted to stay on for "short-term" duty. Don decided to put in a request for "temporary" assistance. Not too many people knew, but that was how he got three of his other deputies. Don could justify acquiring the extra deputy because the population had increased in this area. More homes being built and families growing. He had a sixth sense about people and knew that the temporary status would soon become permanent. This kid had savvy. Don knew that he would be a good addition to his team. (Don always thought of his deputies as a "team.") Carl had a wife, a new baby, and this would be an ideal place to raise a family.

"Nice big brother. Sounds like he's a user."

"User?"

"Yeah! A people user's the kind of person that hasn't got what it takes to do things for themselves. They're either lazy, afraid someone might find out they don't know how, or they're a coward to do whatever it is. So they bully somebody else into doing it for them. Bully's usually use anger to cover their apprehensions. They're usually very possessive too. Like losing control of his ex-wife is making him crazy, so he strikes out at her. Cowards do their dirty work when nobody else is around. Like the way he ran when Tom came home, then he went back later, when nobody else was home to tear her house up."

"Sounds like you've got a handle on Gary all right. 'Bully' and 'coward' describes him perfectly," Don complimented him.

"I've always been a study of human nature. I got good grades in psychology. My parents wanted me to be a doctor, but I'm not the type of person to nurse rich people out of a nervous breakdown over a hangnail. It's not my thing."

"Well good for you! I'm pleased to hear you say that. I'm kind of the same way myself. I'm into the understanding part, but not the curing part of it."

"Yes sir," Carl said with a smile not easily removed. He liked this man. Sheriff Wilson reminded him of his uncle Tony, a man that he'd always looked up to.

"Well, Deputy! Let's get this show on the road," Don said, waving the tow truck forward. "Let's get this picked up, and in the trunk of your patrol car. Tell the driver to wait. As soon as we finish up here, we'll follow his truck to the station."

"Yes, sir."

. . .

When Tom arrived at the house, he found most of his furniture (what was left of it) on the lawn. His mattress and a few other items were in two of the larger pickup trucks.

Lilly was carrying a box of damaged photographs out to her truck. "Hey, Tom. I thought I'd see if I can salvage these pictures. I've got a computer program that will help me fix these. They're mostly just wrinkled, but some have little tears and cuts from the broken glass. That large painting of your parents won't be very hard to fix either."

"Wow! This is wonderful. I thought they were history. You can do that?"

"She sure can," Howard said. "This young lady has magic fingers when it comes to an artistic challenge. You won't even know anything happened to them when you get them back. You should see some of the things she has created."

"I'd like to see some of your art work sometime. I'm getting an insurance settlement, so let me know how much everything costs. I haven't told Becka how badly everything was damaged. This is going to mean a lot to her. Most of these pictures are irreplaceable. Thank you so much."

"Not a problem. This will give me an excuse to get back to my computer. I love doing this kind of stuff," Lilly said. "Howard, would you please get the large portrait and wrap it in a sheet or something, and bring it out to my truck?"

"Sure! I'll bring it right out," he said and walked into the house with Tom.

Joanne was in the kitchen. She had cleaned up the mess and was making lunch for everybody. She had stopped by the store on the way over. There were two large plates of sandwiches, two or three different kinds of chips on the table, a large pot of soup on the stove, and cans of soda and beer in the refrigerator. "Joanne! You're a miracle worker," Tom said as he entered the kitchen. "It looks like nothing happened in here. And you cooked too! Look at all this food."

"Not much cooking really. Just the soup. Your can opener works nicely." Joanne blushed. "Hardworkin' people gotta eat. It's the least I could do."

"The soup smells good. I haven't had anything to eat since . . . I think it was yesterday. Do you mind?" he said as he picked up one of the sandwiches. "Mmm! This is good."

"Not at all. That's what they're there for."

"I didn't realize that I was hungry until I came in here. This is delicious. Thank you," he said, grabbing a handful of chips. "I'm going to see what everybody else is doing."

"That's fine, dear. The soup should be ready in about fifteen minutes." "This is great . . . Thanks," Tom said and went back into the living room. George Foster from "The Village" had sent his two oldest boys, Jerry and Danny, over to help. Tom knew them from his martial arts classes. Two of his best students. They both had dust pans and were sweeping up the broken glass off the carpet. "It's nice of you guys to help out. Thank you," Tom praised.

"You're welcome. But there's a lot of tiny pieces that we can't get out," Jerry told him.

"This will tear up the inside of your vacuum cleaner. What do you want us to do?" Danny asked.

"Just do the best you can with the brooms. I sure hope the insurance company will replace it. If not, I have a friend that can do it for me. He has a carpet outlet in town."

Sara and Howard's wife, Irene Bluefeather, were scrubbing the bathroom when Tom stuck his head in the door. "This looks good, ladies. Thank you."

"You're welcome, Tom," they both said together. They did this quite often. Everybody teased them about being twins. They were about the same age and could pass for sisters.

Lilly walked up behind him. "Is there anything else I can do, Tom?" "I don't know. Let's go look at the bedroom."

"I saw the wall. He really did a job on it. I just hope we can get the lipstick off. Sometimes paint will soak up color. Especially an oil base like lipstick. We might have to repaint it," Lilly informed him.

Larry and Jerry Flowers were getting ready to wash the wall. They had scrub brushes and rags in a bucket.

"Tong!"

"Wait a minute, guys." Lilly said. "Lipstick is tricky stuff to get off of anything. What are you using?"

"Well! We've got bleach and scouring powder," Jerry told her.

Larry started to scrub a small area to try it out. It smeared and made a circle of Passion Red lipstick under the brush. "Oh great! This is only making it worse," he said.

"Tong!"

"Here. Let me try," Lilly offered. "You're right. This is not working," she agreed after trying unsuccessfully to wipe the red circle off the wall.

"Tong!"

She took the bucket and said, "Let me see what kind of cleaners Becka has in the kitchen. I'll be right back."

In the kitchen, she said, "Mmm! It really smells good in here, Joanne."

"Thanks. The soup is done. You can tell everybody that it's time to eat whenever they're ready."

"OK! But first I want to see what kind of cleaners Becka has under the sink." She dumped the bucket into the sink and filled it with warm water and set it on the floor in front of the open cabinet door. With her back to Joanne, she touched the containers one by one.

"Tong!"

"Tong!"

"Tong!"

"Ting!"

"Ahh! Here we go," she said and poured a small amount of dish detergent into the water. She put her hand in the water and swirled it around to make suds.

"Ting! . . . Ting! . . . Ting! . . . Ting!" The crystal enhanced the cleaning solution.

"This should do just fine," she said as she picked up the bucket and returned to the bedroom. "Here try this."

When they wrung out the rags and scrubbed the wall, it became sparkling clean. "What is this stuff? It's working really good."

"Ting!"

"Just a painter's trick. Learned it from a friend of my grandpa's," she fudged.

"Thanks! This is coming off faster than I'd thought it would," Jerry said. "Good! Joanne's got lunch ready for everybody."

"Bless her heart. I'm starving! Moving all that furniture used up my breakfast real fast," Howard said. "Come on, everybody."

Nobody wanted to leave. They were fascinated with the way the wall was cleaning up.

. . .

About ten minutes later, everyone arrived in the kitchen. "There you are. Help yourselves, there's plenty of everything."

Everybody was sitting around after lunch and talking when Don arrived. "This place looks a lot better than it did last night."

"Yes! These nice people have done so much that I'll never pay everyone back," Tom said.

"Don't worry, Tom! Friends are supposed to help each other. I'm sure there will be favors exchanged in the future," Larry said. "Just hope that it doesn't take something this bad to get us together again. My brother really screwed up this time."

Everyone agreed.

"Have you had lunch yet, Don?" Lilly asked.

"Not yet."

"Joanne has fixed a very nice meal for everyone. There's some left in the kitchen," she told him.

"Thanks! I'll be right back," he said and left the room.

"Joanne, would you come with me? I need to talk to you."

"Sure! I'll be right there." When she got to the kitchen, Don was tasting his soup. "Get yourself a sandwich too. I'm going to put these in plastic bags before the bread dries out."

"Mmm! This is good. Thank you!" he said and cleared his throat. "The community is having a Halloween Barn Dance this weekend. I was wondering if you would like to attend with me."

"Well! That's nice of you. I would be delighted. Thank you!" She blushed.

"No! Thank *you,* and it would be an honor for me to introduce you to your new neighbors. Everybody will be there," he said as his own pink cheeks returned their normal color.

"I'm looking forward to it. What time does it start?" she asked. "After it gets dark. Why don't I pick you up about six o'clock?"

"That's fine, but I don't have a costume. I hope that's OK," Joanne fussed.

"Not a problem," he assured her. "Most of the adults don't usually wear costumes. Some do, but we give out prizes to the kids for theirs. It's hard for them to do any 'trick or treating' up here, so we make it up to them with lots of goodies, games, and presents. They all get something, even the little ones. I'm sure you'll have fun."

"Sounds like lots of fun."

"It is. Oh yeah! Bring your appetite. There's going to be a pot luck buffet."

"What can I bring?"

"Just yourself. First timers are always guests. You can show off your cooking at the Christmas Party. I'm hoping you'll accept me as your escort to that one too."

"Let's see how this party goes, first. You may not want to."

"I don't think there's a chance of that, but I'll ask again when time comes. You may not want to go with me for some reason. I promise to behave myself." He smiled.

Joanne smiled back. "OK! It's a deal. You can ask me later. I don't know if I like socializing. I haven't done it in so long."

They shook hands and goose flesh ran up both of their arms. Both being a little flustered, they released their hands quickly.

EPILOGUE
FIVE MONTHS LATER

Joanne and Don were an item. Their children had come to visit during the Christmas holiday. They all got along like one big happy family.

Joanne had helped Larry reupholster the furniture that he had repaired. Tom and Becka had a healthy baby boy, which they named Donald Thomas Freeman.

Larry and Susan were to be married in June. The whole community was helping with their plans. Everyone had a change of heart after Larry testified against his brother in court. Now they understood. Larry wasn't the troublemaker that his brother forced him to be.

The word had spread that Larry did good work. People from all over the area were keeping him so busy with odd jobs that his boss Danny Lovett set up a corner for him in the hardware store. He had Lilly make a beautiful sign and mounted it next to the name of the store. Now it said, "LOVETT HARDWARE," and underneath in letters almost as big "LARRY'S CARPENTRY AND REPAIR SHOP." Things were finally going right in Larry's life. Ken and Tillie Johnson, his parents, didn't come to his brother's trial. They didn't spend any more of their money on lawyers either. But they said that they would be at the wedding with bells on. As a wedding gift, they had purchased a small cabin in the area and had given them the deed early so that Larry could fix it up before they moved in. The couple that owned it were moving to Europe and couldn't keep it maintained, so they put it up for sale.

Lilly was making more of her beautiful pieces of art. Now that she had the crystal, the work went much faster and easier. Never letting the crystal create anything but asking for help with the things that took a lot of strength.

"Thank you, Grandpa."

"Ting!"

www.ingramcontent.com/pod-product-compliance
Ingram Content Group UK Ltd.
Pitfield, Milton Keynes, MK11 3LW, UK
UKHW041945230426
12048UKWH00008B/140